AF410661

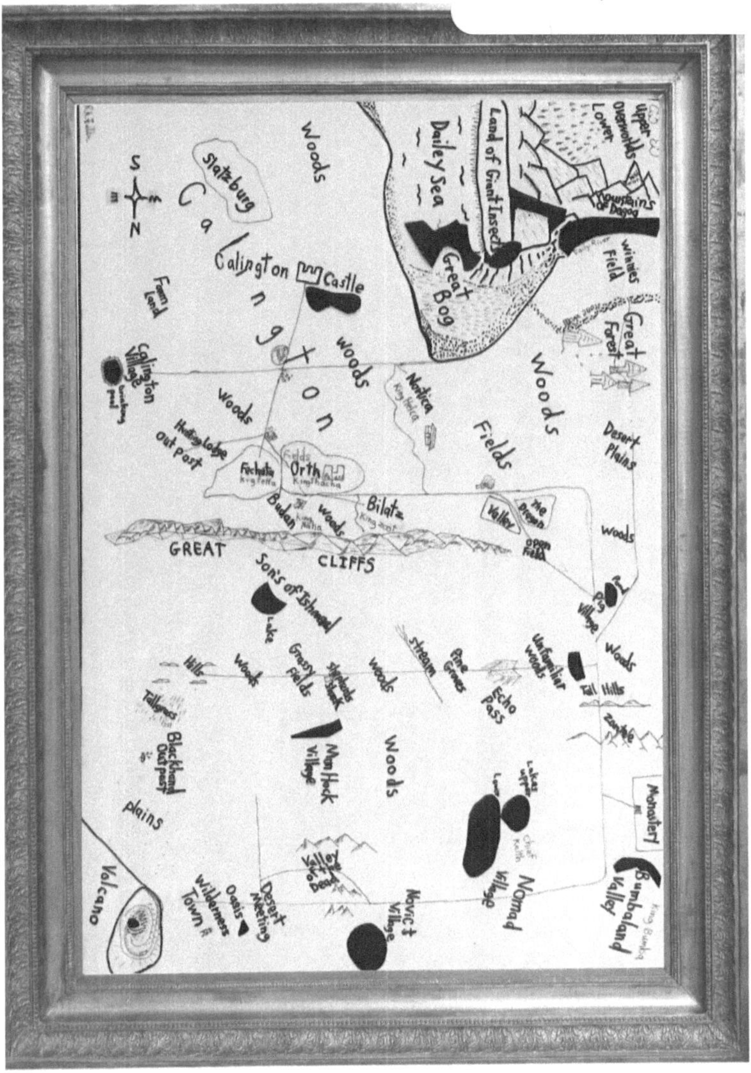

Upper Overworlds
Lower
Mountains of Dagog
Dailey Sea
Land of Giant Insect
Great Bog
Slatzburg
Woods
S
E
N
Calington
Calington Castle
Farm Land
Calington Village
Hunting pool
winnies Field
Great Forest
Desert Plains
Woods
Fields
Nautica King Nata
Hunting Lodge out Post
Fechatia King Teffa
Orth
Kimthatha
Bilata King Sart
Budah King Nata
Woods
GREAT CLIFFS
Valley
the Dream
open field
Woods
P.S village
Son's of Ishmael
Lake
Grassy Fields
Hills
woods
Tall Falls
Blackland Out post
Plains
Volcano
Stream
Pine Groves
Echo pass
Unfamiliar woods
Woods
Tall Hills
Zarsile
Man Hock Village
Woods
Lakai upper
Lower
Chief Keith
Nomad Village
Monastery
Bumbaland Valley
King Bumba
Valley of the Dead
Desert Meeting
Oasis
Wilderness Town
Navic Village

Calington Castle I

Learning to Love the Truth

New Edition

R.A. Feller

ISBN 979-8-9894920-7-7 (paperback)
ISBN 979-8-9894920-6-0 (digital)

Printed in the United States of America

This book is dedicated to those who love to go on quests for the truth and thoroughly enjoy the journey along the way.

Contents

I

$\mathcal{T}$he winds whoosh and spirits dance about in the air saying, *"We seek refuge with conquering thoughts. For us to find a place that we might dwell!*

Live and breathe by single darkened choice. Only to be found amongst the free will of a soul within the entrance of the minds of man."

The black hooves thrash through bright yellow grass glistening in the light of the sun. It is autumn, and the cool air is felt beneath the armor of men. They ride with their king.

Prince Liam rides by his father's side. It is not the sound of the onslaught of the enemy-this doth not bother him-but something stirs within.

A single thought causes Liam to see. *"It is not his purpose to kill anymore."* War doth not seem to be a part of who he now is. Agreeing with his thought that tells him, *"Perhaps, truly there is a better way."* He decides to find out!

Although well-trained for battle, an inner voice of light continues. Hearing it over and over, it tells him, *"This is not the direction of his destiny."*

Just before the king's army engages in combat, Liam finally hears it out loud 'til it becomes a shout of his own. "Father, I take leave!" Liam then breaks from the ranks turning back.

Other thoughts, dragons invade his mind as he turns: *"Where are you going?—The men need your leadership."* He rides on. *"You'll never be able to face your father. Some may die because of this selfish choice,"* and then an overwhelming thought, as a final resounding blow attempts to invade his mind: *"They'll call you a coward!"*

Unmoved, Liam continues to ride away. He has been in battles before. The stories and glories of war have been drummed into his head since youth. Yet, have they become a sound that would drown out all other growth from his life as well?

There was an incomplete image in his mind. A missing thread or two as it were, which kept him from seeing the whole design of the pattern. Or, are the other threads that now have his focus an even more vital part of the design than he had once thought? Threads that were needed to support the fabric of all reality fully?

Nervously, Liam wipes the sweat from his brow as he lets loose on the reins. His horse begins to trot. Just as he leaves the lines, while making peace with his decision, he feels a burning sensation.

Struck by an arrow, Prince Liam experiences a deep penetrating pain and begins to fall from the side of his horse.

Haugh! I abruptly awake and find myself sitting up, taking quick, heavy breaths. My room slowly comes in sight, and as I adjust to my usual surroundings, my focus starts to shift.

"This has been the third time I have had this dream."

I am no stranger to battle, but the thought of not being able to fight against this nightmare has been most disturbing.

Slipping out of bed, my feet touch the damp, sobering floor. I go to the window and have a look, trying to change the mood I'm in.

It is early in the morn and the stars still hang, piercing the veil of a dark night sky. The smooth stones beneath my feet have now become uncomfortably wet. Upon drying them, I put on some boots and venture out of my chamber to dimly torch-lit corridors.

Haunted by my dream, I make my way to my Brother Edward's room and knock upon his door.

While I wait, I wonder if I'm doing the right thing in coming to him. But I must confess that he is the more stable of the two of us these days.

Our father's unpredictable behavior has grown increasingly worse. Being the eldest, I have taken the brunt of it - which has been most draining.

I go to knock a second time and Edward opens suddenly. I jump back with surprise, which surprises him. Now, we are both very much awake.

Edward finds me holding my right hand in a loose fist up to my heart. My breaths are yet heavy, and I'm now slouched in a slightly forward position.

"Liam, is everything all right?"

I ponder my thoughts and answer what is told me, "Yes—I'm not so sure?"

"You'd better come in."

We sit down on his bed, and then I tell him of my dream. "Have you told this to anyone else?"

"Nowhere else to go since the priests have gone. Father taking up that cup, drinking 'til his eyes are red, and now..."

"He has become a wild animal lately, hasn't he? And I know peace has been difficult to find, Liam. Especially with his unruly fits and uncontrollable rage!"

"Before the priests left, I am under impression they thought he had an evil spirit."

"Now the deeper the pit, the longer the Great One's arm is able to reach into it!"

"Well spoken, Edward. We must be aware of harboring resentments during these times...*or* things might...get rather confusing?"

There is a long pause before my brother's reply, which leads me to believe he keeps a secret. Edward continues, "I've *heard* the priests are in waiting, praying day and night for the appointed time of the deliverer."

"Who is this deliverer to be?"

"Father's drinking has really gotten to you, my poor brother."

Believing he may have offended me, Edward pauses. After he sees I do not react, my brother feels compelled to continue.

"I think he's gotten to us all, Liam. No one can get very close to him anymore."

"Tell me more of our *deliverer*; I need to hear it, particularly at times like these."

"Well, no one knows when He is to come, but my hope is...at the appointed time, he'll bring back purity to the people and restore the kingdom with His wise words and actions."

"Boy, I'd sure like to meet him. Why, I'd even settle for a priest right now just to find out what my dream means."

"The fact you are next in line for the throne, having had the exact same dream three times in a row. This could mean...the Great One is not only trying to speak to you, but have a message for all our people.

I will break my silence. I believe our queen and mother knows where the priests are."

"Now, how do you know all this and I do not?"

"I happened by at the time of their departure, overhearing bits and pieces of conversation from the priests of the Order.

Where they're staying, I do not know, but I did hear she could send them prayer requests and something about taking courage. For the Great One is able to see you through all adversity. Work all things out for the good of those who love Him, and to take heart for they'd be praying for her."

"I wish I could have been there. If only there was something I could have done to stop this!"

"Like what? You know it is not your time to rule... sad, but true."

The birds begin to chirp out in the garden. Edward suddenly comes to the realization, "Hey, it'll be morn soon!"

Then I realize it too, as we say together. "Mother always prays at the dais at sunrise!"

"I will go to her, tell her of my quest, and find out the meaning of my dream!"

"Don't forget to dress first and let me know what happens!"

I take leave of my brother with great excitement. My heart soars as my thoughts begin to race. The reality of what is happening starts to move me while sinking in.

"I know I must be calm to see clearly. As there is no telling what will unfold before me. 'Do I go back to sleep? No, I'll only bounce out of bed.' Let me get dressed for travel and go to meet mother in prayer at morn.'

It is *still* before sunrise. All is quiet, as a fine summer's haze fills the night air, signifying yet another uncomfortably humid day to come on the morrow.

I pause momentarily by the frog pond in the courtyard as the moon shines down upon the water amongst its lilies.

My focus shifts, the moon now gives light upon the many steps throughout the entrance of the great hall.

Beams of moonlight come through the castle window. Upon entering the hall, all sounds of the croaking frogs fade way.

Meeting with mother in prayer at morn has my full attention.

I pass through moonbeams and come to the opening of a long corridor. Torches now light my way.

For some reason, memories from my past...thoughts I have not had in years surface; they come and swarm my mind. I continue to walk.

I recall at age four, how my mother's growing belly told tale. *"I was not going to be an only child anymore.'* After my fifth birthday, mother gave birth to Edward.

I was excited about having a younger brother from the start. Later on, when I saw how much attention he was getting, I wasn't so sure anymore.

I approach some long, smooth, stone steps that meet with the wall, as they curve to where they begin their ascension. More thoughts come, *"I remember the attention my brother was getting was no fault of his own. I was able to draw closer to him after this."*

I watched my brother grow from babe unto child. Boy to man. I wondered all the while–what was this friendly little fellow going to become? Though watching him made me forget I was getting older, too.

Then all at once it hit me, *"By divine right, I was next in line for the throne. I knew it in the back of my mind really, but why me and not Edward? I am glad the Great One had ordained it this way. 'Great One, priests,' oh my, my mother's throne!"*

I marvel at how easily I've become sidetracked from my present focus. "But whose spirit is there to follow that will truly keep me at peace? Then, I remember the facts of what I've been taught and weigh them against the way all things are coming apart lately. I don't understand why the priests had to go." Then a darkness invades.

"Now, I'm just not so sure of what to believe anymore."

The steps are large and wide beneath my feet. There are several high windows set within the walls that curve along with them. I climb the stair and moonbeams mix with the haze of the heavy summer air–while illumination from the torches, hanging on the walls, add to the heat.

Beads of sweat roll down my face, adding to the discomfort, but I pay them no mind as I am nearing my destination.

Continuing up the steps, oddly, even more thoughts come, but these sharpen my focus. First of my father who ran the kingdom, *"Which at one time he did so well. Everybody liked him. For he was fair with everyone.*

Standing for what was right, everyone knew his faith, being a proven man of principle.

Uncommon to his now present nature, noticed upon his return from one of his trips." Now ruling with drink, the golden goblet had become commonplace in hand.

"How distant we've become." I noticed it with his subjects, too.

"Although I search, I can no longer find place within his life.

This causes me to bear a pain of my own, along with many of those at court. Why, weeks have gone by without even a word from him.

There was no time for family either. Only the cordial royal doldrums of the roles we now play.

Turning to prayer lately, I've learned that I must be more patient with father.

Perhaps the Great One will reveal to me what must be done in this situation. I must—I will wait upon Him, then the timing will be right for me to act."

Due to my inadequate amount of sleep this night, I become drowsy while continuing to walk up the stairs. I actually have thoughts about stopping for a rest. *"No, I must go on!"*

I push through my thoughts 'til out of mind, but as I do, others come to take their place.

"'What to do about the family situation?' I hated what was becoming of things. My father continues to drain the life out of everyone. Especially poor mother. Yet, I watched him with my brother, how he held him as a child.

Hadn't he held me when I was two or three? Rock me in his arms, bounce me on his knee, speak softly to me with the love of his heart?

Then there were the hunting trips.

Edward's first ride upon a horse with us all. It was his arrow that landed the deer that day. How we all laughed as it roasted.

We were so proud, so joyously close, my father and brother, but where was I? It was so long ago. If it had not been for Edward, I would have been isolated, as if in jail.

He sensed a secret, but out of respect, he'd never ask.

Why all these thoughts? And why so sluggish on these stairs? Am I under a spell or in a dream?"

I remember a conversation that Edward and I had, *"What we would look for in a bride? We would have fun telling of whom the Great One would bring into our lives.*

One time, I caught two servants embraced in a kiss. I looked away, but evidently this thought stayed with me, dimming my senses within soul of mind.. For when at a feast, my eyes caught sight of a young maiden; a daughter of a nobleman and her eyes were looking back at mine. We drew near, then closer still, our lips drawn to each other like a moth to a flame. Suddenly, she turned her head, "You don't understand love the same way I do."

"But I'm really not like this, I only copied from what I saw my servants doing!"

"'I like your honesty, but you should not practice what you do not understand.' How I did enjoy her light!"

Whatever it is, then leaves me as I hear the sound of shouts. Father's voice next clears my mind.

I'm found more unmoved from my intent, my motion is steady and upward.

On the ascension my focus returns; this time with a sense of urgency.

My footsteps do not seem to be quite quick enough. As lacking in sleep, I find my exhilaration quickly turn to fatigue.

I round the turn and wipe the sweat from my brow. Their voices grow exceedingly louder and angry. *"Next, things get too quiet as if calm before storm."*

I hear them again, my father the king and queen mother, speaking less than royal worth.

"Henry, you don't look so good. Have you been up all night drinking?" My father's impatient voice was that of strong wine talking.

"I'm sick and tired of your meddlesome advice, which I like a fool always take. But no more! Because of you, we might be at war again–now where's my pretty golden goblet?!"

I hear him fill it, then a thud of an empty cask shoved to the floor. I next hear my mother lose her patience, "My fault, can't you see what your drinking is doing to us and our kingdom? What has happened to the man I married? You're not even fit to be ruler of yourself, let alone a kingdom anymore!"

There is a darkness growing in the atmosphere and I quicken my pace, as thoughts tell me their argument is about to get out of control...

"I can't believe they're fighting like this, and the way father has been behaving lately, anything is liable to happen. I have to put a stop to it!" lights my mind.

My steps are heard echoing off the walls of the passageway. Then a rather strange thing happens. Although the air had been flowing against my face, all of a sudden I feel a wind pass from behind. The torches capture my attention as I watch them flicker on the breeze.

I ponder how peculiar this is. Then immediately after, I hear my father's angry and unstable voice get violent, "You can't talk to me like that you wrinkled wench. I know about those lines you hide beneath your make-up."

"How dare you!"

I next hear her footsteps advance toward him, and the sound of something being lifted off the table between their thrones.

"Give me my cup, wench!"

Rounding the turn, the picture becomes complete. I see my father charge toward my mother, but as soon as she puts down the goblet of gold, he stops his advance. I let out a sigh of relief.

Approaching, I go unnoticed. Then my hands go up as father suddenly lets out a loud insane laugh, which turns to a rage filled snarl.

"Take my cup would you. I'll teach you!"

Fear grips my heart and I freeze–Father stirs uneasily 'til quick and without warning he strikes my mother across her face with the full force of his backhand. "Nooo!" I cry out watching helplessly as she falls over backward from the dais, rolling down its steps. Finally, she comes to a rest by my feet.

My mother's body appears lifeless. I check and see that she still breathes. Then as I arise, my father's eyes lock with mine. I fill with anger, restrained only by my love of God.

"Father, how could you?!"

He looks away, taking a gulp from his golden goblet, then speaks sternly to me in a loud voice, "You'll say nothing of this to anyone or you will be banished, Liam! Is that understood?"

I raise my hands with clenched fists and collapse to my knees. My breaths are yet heavy with the back of my fingers before my face. Suddenly, fear grips me. The seemingly great weight of his unruly authority in this situation drives my mind dim.

I peer out over my knuckles, answering the stench of my father's breath in shock. "Y-yes sire, I understand!"

"Now, go inform the royal healer that our queen has stumbled and fallen upon the dais."

"A-at once, sire!"

I take leave, apprehensive to abandon mother with this king. *"Yet what choice do I have? I rise up to leave, but oddly enough a part of me feels like it is being left behind.*

It causes me to feel awkward, like I am being pushed into the shadows of a broken image." More thoughts come to convince, *"How I'd get used to the changes around here... and that I was next in line to reign—How if I was to keep my head somehow, I could make a difference in the future. After all, my turn will come to wear the crown; I'll be all right",* These voices of thought manage to block what I am really feeling for the time being. So I lay it all to rest, not yet realizing the impact it shall have–

For this is to be my burial: I'm to be subtly covered over with many winds of thought, lying spirits upon my mind where buried now I'll be 'til I be no more.

Now with darkness blinding my sight, a compulsion quickly drives me to find the way to our healer. Time seems to stand still on this short journey.

Inside, an uneasiness floats about my heart. I am concerned for mother, I do not wish her left in present danger. Speedily she must be tended, as there's no telling what this king is capable of.

Relentless swarms, troubling thoughts, run down my head to heart and tear at all emotion from inside. A chill within my feelings suggests I go numb, as a swirl snaps them into a whirlwind, which swims about my soul.

I next arrive at our family friend's chamber. Seldom is he moved from his peace. The healer picks up on my anxiety while looking on. He decides to test my spirit by slowly placing herbs into a pouch. I try and persuade him to come at once, yet he reminds, "All is done in the Great One's time."

II

Step by step, after step by step, the king walks through the twilight haze. A blank stare holds him as he stops just before his fallen queen.

Lowering his head, he sees her crumpled body and denies the full impact of the situation.

"Mary...Mary...Mary! Would you get up? What'd you have to go and fall down for?"

He raises his head and continues, "It's just like you to never finish a good argument, and as for you sire ..." raising his goblet of gold, "What you need–is a drink!"

Finding his cup empty, he staggers towards another cask of strong wine. I next enter with the healer, we both go to my mother's side. Aiding him in turning her body, a mark is discovered upon her face. The healer examines her and further discovers how serious her injuries are.

"What has happened, sire?"

"The queen lost her footing and fell. Will she be all right?"

"She will never walk again, her back is broke."

Tears fill my eyes upon hearing the news. In disbelief I ask, "Are you sure?"

"Yes, I'm afraid so."

"When will she awake?"

"It's hard to say, so many bruises." Looking at the bruise upon her face, "How peculiar this one is?" The king responds clearing his throat, "Liam, summon the guard for a detail to carry our queen to her chambers!"

"Yes, sire."

I watch for a moment as my father and king staggers about. He looks to fill his goblet of gold–with yet another drink.

Without my mother's temperance to keep him in check, what will we do now? Fleeing for fear of his now impatient temperament, I quickly find my way out, grieving my mother's very present wounds. The healer looks on surmising the situation, I pass him by.

Speedily, I seek out the guard and give instruction. My sense of urgency finally leaves me, and hereafter for a brief moment I find peace.

Now that the guards know to meet with the healer, I go back to my room and collapse on my bed.

"Oh Great One, what is to happen now? Have mercy upon us." I then doze off to sleep just short of despair.

Later at morn, I'm awakened by a hand upon my shoulder. It startles me. My brother Edward questions, "Have you heard?"

I'm relaxed, now that I know it is my brother, and reply in a half conscious state of mind as I sit up, "You mean about mother?"

"What do you know?"

I see that I have let my tongue slip, "I'd rather not talk, it is really upsetting."

"She's my mother too, you know?"

"Oh, very well then!"

Realizing I could not tell him the truth, I cough to collect my thoughts before continuing, "She was in the middle of a heated argument with the king..."

"You mean, father?"

"No, I mean the king. He's no longer a father to me."

"That must have been quite an argument."

"Well, he frightened her, and backing away she tripped in her gown. Mother then fell on the dais stair."

"Father said that she stumbled."

"Tripped, stumbled, what's the difference?"

"What's the matter, Liam?...Something else happened that you're not telling me. I know you!"

He suspects I'm lying. I hear a whisper, *"You will be banished..."*

"It's just, I was there and felt as if I could have done something to stop it. Okay?"

"It's all right, I'll leave you be...The healer says she has amnesia..."

"She's awake! Oh thanks be to the Great One!"

"She knows not who she is, but the healer recommends we visit and tell her. when the time comes of the oh so many details of her life.

He hopes it will get her to remember at least parts of her identity."

"Edward still suspects. I know him too well to give up that easily.

'Another thought comes, *'I'm going to mother.'"*

"I'll come with you! Perhaps her seeing the two of us together will be a stronger witness, which will greater aid in placing her memory back together sooner."

"I want to go alone!"

"I'm distancing myself from him and he knows it. Now what'll I say?" Then a clever thought enters my mind and I choose to use it, "Edward, it's just that I want to be alone with her. Please understand this."

"For a minute there I thought I was with father. Oops, I mean the king!" My heart feels a tear in our relationship. He turns and starts walking away...Letting more thoughts take over, I do nothing to stop it.

In my mind I hear the deception, *"He'll come around. Don't worry,"* but in my heart of hearts I sense that I am going numb.

"I feel out of place here, something has happened to me. I don't belong—or at least I've become aware of the fact that something lives inside of me, which dims my mind that doth not belong.

I'm found to hide in the shadows of only a portion of who I am, and there's no escaping the lie that now tries to blind me from my own identity. I try to strengthen myself by taking solace at mother's side.

I soon recognize, unless I face the king at some point in the future I may actually cease to exist.

I hold off on seeing mother now. For I fear, if she should recognize any changes in me, it would break her heart. So, I find out from others what is going on with her. I hear she's starting to gain moments of recall, but then fades back into forgetfulness.

"Could I hold the key to unlock her mind and bring her back to us, or would the shock of the light of what has happened damage her further by going to fast? I know I must wait, but it is...difficult!"

I'm a stranger now to my brother and stay in my room or go on long rides to further avoid the lie that is becoming my life. *"I see myself in the mirror, and looking into my eyes I see a stranger looking back at me; a glaze has entered my eyes."*

"Noooo!"

"I can't. I shall stand for this no longer." I turn and start to take deep, heavy breaths. A kind voice next enters my mind, *"It doth not have to be this way!"*

I know now, I'm worth nothing like this. Another thought comes that is just as lovely. Then all the darkness that has invaded my soul takes leave while I raise a fisted hand. *"By the Great One's grace it is time to see the king!"*

The sun sets as I approach his chambers. Royal guard stand their post beside the door. Knocking, I am bid to come in and find the king sitting upon a stone bench on the balcony. He admires the colors of the sky at eve. I stand near him on one side with his golden goblet resting next to him on the bench on the other.

Noticing him to be between the two subjects that hold his affection, the question comes to mind, *"Which one will the sun go down on?"*

"Father, much has happened. I feel I must talk with you!"

"Come sit down Liam, and say what need be said."

Addressing him while still standing, he pats the bench with his hand. I am in disbelief as he notices not where I am, through his glazed over-stare. Angrily, I raise my voice, "The best I can say is–as revealed to me by the Spirit of the Great One-my vision has been disrupted. And not only mine, but our beloved kingdoms.

We have come under attack by a dark spirit!" He now gives me his full attention.

"I further believe it has come upon us through your drinking–and if the priests were here they would stand behind me, I'm sure."

"Nonsense! There's nothing to this, Liam. I just have an occasional drink!"

"Father, ever since you've returned from the peace summit, that cup has never left your side. Your drinking has almost choked out who we are and all held dear I discover to be slipping away!"

"What's all this you're talking about?"

"The lie that keeps me from being banished from this kingdom has caused me to take on another identity. It has banished me from my own soul, and this vision I can stand for no longer...

It has been like hiding behind walls when I talk with others from court, and these walls have been growing to imprison me!"

"Have you said anything to anyone else?"

"I'm saying it now. You father, shall remain in prison if you don't protect the honor of this kingdom and our family relationships.

Go to the proconsul out of respect for honest love, as a lack of truth always invites further darkness. Father, report the account of what has happened about mother. Now!"

"They'd say I'm a drunkard and question my judgment. Would this not bring division amongst my subjects? Everyone knows that a kingdom divided against itself cannot stand. It would never do!"

"There's division now, and as you keep sweeping things under the rug, you shall have no more room to cover the pile. It will remain seen by all.

Besides, have you not heard, 'A double minded man is unstable in all his ways?'

Father, while you get better, I can help you rule."

"Share my throne? What are the other alternatives?"

"I go to the proconsul and report what's happening, if you don't! Father, can't you see that everyone would be encouraged by your desire to get well? It will be a show of strength to ask for help!"

"My son, my boy, my prince! I only seek a simple favor, consider everything I've done. Couldn't you just look the other way? Is that too much to ask?"

"It's not you who asks! For my father would never address me in such a manner. Without honor we have nothing. Yet, even now we receive the Great One's grace. For as He knocks on the door to all hearts, it is He who vindicates.

Now is the hour at hand! I've been raised up under the Great Ones authority to tell you, 'You're not hearing His voice any longer, you've surrendered to second best!'

What has happened to the excellent Spirit that had governed your soul before the drinking started?"

"Guards! Guards! Guards!" I hear them as they approach.

"Father, there's no need to call out the guard on me. For in doing so, you're not only betraying our kingdom, but yourself."

"Am I the one who is trapped here, or you?"

Suddenly I find myself being seized, "I will call upon the Great One day and night if necessary, 'til you're delivered from this affliction!"

"No need to pray for me, Liam. I'm fine. Save your prayers for yourself, as you are the one who is afflicted."

"You're my king. Whenever I pray for you, all are covered. Let it be known, it is my heart's desire for all to be well!"

Following the king's instructions, the guards are informed not to listen. I've a treasonous tongue, so they've been told.

In addition, I hear the king say that I'm to be locked away in the high tower. My spirit wells up within me in outcry, "My lord. My king. Father, don't do this!"

There's such a cold spirit at work. I watch as it keeps my father away from the warmth of the light of truth. He next replies with a heart of stone.

"It is done!"

As I'm being led out the door, I hear a final command, "Post no visitors!" I'm stunned at first, and fight off my emotions while being marched away, but as they get the better of me I shout, "I'll have more room to move about in the tower than you will in all of Calington!"

I am found at the doorway of despair while escorted away. Then the Great One speaks to my mind... something about the walls. *I have a plan!*

Now the thought comes to me as to why the priests left the kingdom…*"Their faith really doth lay in the deliverer to bring about change. He must be sent by the Great One!*

He's the one to set all things to order again." Then I know and agree with my thoughts. It will not be by the power of the hands of a mere man.

I must find the priests and learn more of what is to come. I start to get butterflies in my stomach as I'm escorted towards the tower, but then the Great One's confidence enters my heart. Next, in an astounding moment, I feel my strength return. Resolved in earnest, I know who I am purposed to be in spirit and in truth!

However, when it is almost time to put the Great One's plan into effect I start to waiver again. *"If you were ever to be with me, be with me now, oh Great One."*

I start to cough, as if in spasm. Then leaning slightly forward I fall into the wall, as though trying to regain my balance.

The guard tells me, "Move along," but it's too late. For I am already in position.

Suddenly, slipping up my arm, I remove the torch from its place with one hand, then turn its holder with the other. As the wall slides open, I hear the other guard shout out with surprise, "What are you doing?"

Quickly, I disappear behind the closing wall, leaving the guards in a frenzy behind me. They immediately try to figure out what next to do, but without the torch they are left in the dark.

"I can't see a thing," one guard utters. "Go down there and get another torch, the king will have our hides if we can't at least get this wall open."

The queen lays in bed. Mother's personal servant pours water before helping her to drink. Suddenly, there's a peculiar sound and the wall creeks, slanting open near the bookcase. The water cup tumbles to the floor. After placing my torch in a holder, I pop my head out and meet with my mother's stern eye.'

"Liam, how many times have I told you never to enter my chambers this way?"

The servant girl responds excitedly. "She remembers you!"

"Of course I remember him. I know my first born son!" Sending the girl for the healer, I rush to my mother's side.

"Mother, there's been an accident. Father struck you, he'd been drinking, you quarreled..."

"Liam, our only hope is for you to find the Great One's deliverer and bring Him here."

"But how will I find Him?"

"Ask our Great One to guide by His mercy."

"Mother, where are the priests?"

"Oh Liam, how good of you to come." She then starts to doze, "My first...born...son."

"Mother, what must be done?" ...*She said to call upon the Great One*, "Great One, please help. Hear me! I must find the priests. I know time is short, please help me find them?"

Losing patience, I begin to shake my mother. "You've got to hear me!"

"Go easy on her, lad. Forcing can do damage." Startled, I turn my head. The servant has returned with the healer.

"I believe your majesty will be pleased to know that the priests are beyond the Tall Hills in the Mountains of Zantee. Now go in peace."

I almost shout for joy, but am reminded by a thought that I'm being sought after by the king's personal guard, so I whisper loudly instead, "Praise be to the Great One!"

The king looks over the stone wall in the corridor where I disappeared.

"Hmmm, the secret passageways? He'll be very hard to catch unless...The queens chambers!"

My father looks to the guard while scheming and addresses them, "I've a confession to make."

The sergeant of the guard gives answer, "What's this all about, majesty?"

"I've tried to cover up for Prince Liam. I fear the queen's accident may have harmed his mind. It would only upset him further if he saw her now.

It was for his own safety I was having him locked away. Let us go quickly to the queen, as I do not believe Liam has taken my counsel to stay away from her.

So, 'til we grab him, humor him in what he says."

They rush towards the queen's chambers and upon reaching her door, the king comes to a halt; his guard falls in line behind. King Henry knocks at the door, but there is no answer. So he pushes the door ajar and peers inside. "Mary? Mary, I've come to look in on you, 'Are you feeling any better?'"

A familiar calm and soothing tone of voice is heard.

"Why don't you come in and see for yourself, your majesty?" are the words noted by the kind, gentle, and yet patient family friend, known well to all.

The king then swings the door wide open. Both the healer and servant girl are revealed, sitting, not far from the queen's bed.

Entering the room, the king and his men find their way before the queen, whose countenance has become aglow.

"Why are you checking in on me with guards?"

"We were just passing by and I thought–Why are you questioning me?"

A look of horror suddenly overtakes my mother's face at the sound of the king's voice.

"My legs, I can't feel my l-e-g-s! No! No! No!"

The queen peels back the covers and finds she cannot sit up as well. Letting forth with a chilling scream heard throughout the castle, her outcry is heard by my brother and he becomes alarmed.

The queen faints from the excitement, but then slowly rocks her head from side to side. She starts to moan...Haugh!

Edward enters her chambers and goes right to mother's side.

Stroking back her soft hair, he soothes her with his voice of love, "Shhhhhh! It's ok, it's going to be okay. There, there, now mum."

Edward looks up to the king, "Father what has happened?"

"The queen has rejoined us."

Edward looks back towards mother, "How wonderful!" Tearfully she responds, "I wish, I wish I were dead."

"Now, you mustn't talk that way. What you need is some cheering up. Guard, go and fetch my brother and bring him here."

The king agreeingly points his finger and sends the other guard along with him to help. He then suggests, "Perhaps Prince Liam doth not want to be found. Maybe he just wants to be alone for a while. How would we find him then?"

"I'll talk to you about that later, mum needs us now. Oh, it's so good to have you with us again, mother. Isn't it father?"

"Yes. Yes, of course!"

"I love you so very, very much. I know it's going to be all right!"

"Oh!! Edward, I can't get up. I can't even feel my legs."

"It's good you're talking about it."

"Yes, Ma'am, it is. It's going to take some time, but you'll adjust, your majesty. You'll see." With his re-affirming voice, the healer manages to soothe the queen. She brings herself to tearfully smile.

"Mum, the healer speaks good sense. We're all here for you: father and me and Liam, with all our many subjects. Why, we're even stronger now that you're back again."

Upon hearing my mother's cry throughout the castle, my heart turns to prayer as I know I cannot be there to comfort her.

I've now become estranged within my own castle, but in so doing I sense that everyone will find a deeper purpose. One that the Great One has in store for us all.

III

$\boldsymbol{A}$ hidden door opens within the outside wall of the castle and I meet with the night air.

Emerging, I quickly make it to the drawbridge. A moment later after the guards pass, I quietly cross over and disappear from sight. The trail leads on, which cuts across fields, where it meets with the road. I have taken no horse, figuring I'd be too easily spotted if anyone was to come looking; nothing is left to chance. Although, I probably will not be missed 'til the sun has risen to mid morn.

My pace keeps me at peace while musing the thoughts of my plan. Now hoping to make it at least as far as the Tall Hills, I walk rapidly during the cover of night.

There's a pleasant breeze in the air this eve. Glad I am to have chosen a hooded robe, which I know to keep over my head as to not be recognized.

My main supply on this journey consists of two skins of water carried by straps crisscrossed over my shoulders. A blanket, which is for sleeping, wrapped around some other provisions that are tied to the end of a stubby stick. I carry it slung over my shoulder.

The stars shine brightly in the night sky and I walk to the light of a full moon. My burden is easy, my way has light, and I am not alone; for the Great One's purpose has my heart.

Many thoughts next lead to what I must face lying ahead.

I have not seen the priests for about a year. They only said that a mission needed carrying out for the Great One, and they'd pray for me while gone.

I wonder if they have completed their mission. They say that "The Great One is always with us." I do feel as though He's with me here, even now. I must say, "He doth have me intrigued as to what will happen next."

Walking in full stride, keeping pace, my thoughts get the focus of my attention while approaching a bend in the road by a great rock. "Here I am of such great value to this kingdom, and yet out of step to make a difference. All the training, all the understanding to grasp the situation for better change, yet here I drift like a valuable coin lost at sea. Now, I must wait on a timing that is not of my own..."

All at once, I feel the sensation of a large cool blade sticking uncomfortably in my throat!

"The bundle! Drop the bundle!"

I regrettably let it fall, but what else can I do? Feeling helpless, I come to the conclusion that the Great One must see me through by His strength alone.

Fortunately, this thought manages to restrain me from the strength of my youth. For I had another thought. A choice to take matters into my own hands, which might have brought disaster.

I hear an accomplice pick up my belongings and run off. With knife removed, the other thief takes to flight as well.

I drop to my knees, grieving loss of provision, but then another thought quickly takes hold of my mind. I find myself thanking the Great One for sparing my life.

Next, I am reminded of my purpose, which must be accomplished—and am encouraged by this *Light*.

"I've still both skins of water and the night is still young. Why, I'll have another go of it."

More sober minded, I realize I was so self-involved that it had me blinded as to what was to come next.

I start to see a pattern, which brings understanding. The more I let go of my self-will, with less provision to own, the more room there be to trust the Great One to guide.

You might consider this coincidence, but the minute my mind clears, I reflect upon thoughts of an old hunting lodge.

"It was miles out of the way and would take me past the land of Fechuta, an ally with Orth. A land whose people were always complaining about paying an unjust tax in proportion to the other tribes. They brought it upon themselves as these lands were taken during a war with Calington.

It was the King of Orth who called a Peace Feast; a summit meeting. Father's attending is how I heard about it. At any rate, it had something to do with—the right of protection from our kingdom if they were to pay taxes."

Turning towards Orth, I am met by a wind. More thoughts come to mind that tell me not to go there, but I had an image of the old lodge in my mind first. *"No, I should continue on the road near Orth. 'Oh, what to do?'"*

If only there was a priest around as guide, then I would know what choice to make., 'Wait a minute, let me check my map.' Then I shall know for sure if I can make it to the Tall Hills, near the Mountains of Zantee before sunrise.

'No!' My map was in my parcel that the thieves have stolen. 'Wait!' There are maps at the old lodge, this must be the way to go. How could it be otherwise?"

I walk for what seems a rather long while 'til reaching a sign post. It points the way to Orth, Fechuta, and some other villages.

Without hesitation I turn towards Orth, unaware that at this very moment, I am being watched by a witch who presumes to know all.

Dark spirits bring information by way of image upon her crystal ball.

The witch stands and starts to step in time while chanting in song before Old King Shacha at his palace in Orth.

"Here comes the prince...here comes the prince, at last he is mine...here comes the prince."

The king of Orth becomes rather amused and begins to laugh while she dances.

"Woe ha ha ha hoe! First, father with the golden goblet, and now his son by kiss of death."

The witch halts, "We haven't much time he'll be here soon."

"What would you have me to do?"

"Have your men bring the maid whom is to be poisoned right away."

"You mean the one who's supposed to be my daughter?"

"Do we have any other dead maiden prospects around here?"

Now perturbed, the king points to some of his men. "Do as she says!"

"Help me move this table."

They slide the witch's specially designed table with her crystal ball on it 'til it rests in the corner of the room. It is then covered with a blanket in preparation for what is to come.

"No, too obvious! Have your men bring it up stairs, he must not suspect anything magical in the air or he will not fall for it."

They continue to set up the room, "You've been so secretive about this spell. I want to know more about what is to happen."

"For a spell to work properly, the atmosphere must be kept fresh for its reality to have its full effect. I wasn't so sure how everything was going to quite come together, but now that I have heard from the spirit world with you being a part of the plan, it is time for me to grant your desire. For knowing what will come to pass will increase the spell's strength.

The prince will come by this way and be curious as to whether or not you are planning yet another uprising. He will investigate, after sensing no weapons this will make him more relaxed.

Next, we will recognize him as a weary traveler and show him some hospitality."

"Hospi, what?"

"Let's just say, 'kindness.'"

"I want to kill him now!" the king shouts with gaul.

"Did you not choose to pay me with half of their kingdom?" Looking to her, the king of Orth blurts out a thought, "What happens if I come up with a better plan?"

When Shacha looks up, the king of Orth gets a sense of evil that words cannot describe. He then backs down from the witch's icy stare.

"I'll trust you!"

"Good! Now that you do, would you like to hear the rest of the plan?"

"You have my interest."

"I will play the role of your queen. We'll serve him a hot meal and engage him in good conversation, all the while he'll be testing our spirits.

Next, when we have his confidence with all prearranged, a servant shall enter the room and whisper in my ear. I will then burst out crying and begin to sob. The prince will ask 'What is the matter?' I will tell of how our eldest daughter had just died of a high fever.

Some of your men will carry in the corpse of a beautiful young maiden poisoned for our occasion... Then lain on a table by the window she'll be. If this be the case–for we must wait and see if the moon is in accordance with the position of this room while it be lit. Which we will know, if its beam shows through the window as it be needed for the spell to work.

Should the moon fail to show in this place, we'll have to bring him to her in another room."

"What if he doth not fall for it?"

"He will want to oblige as a matter of common courtesy, bring comfort to us because of my charm.

For while we dine, I will tell the story of a healer who has left a potion that could be given her. This shall test his honor and he will weigh it within his heart. Then filled with pride, the prince will let down his guard just long enough.

His next line of reasoning shall then slip by, as I will tell him it will be of no effect unless she was kissed by the first born son of a king, by chance we've no sons.

Next, we must wait and see what he'll do.

If he kisses her on the lips by the light of a full moon after he pours potion into her mouth, it will cast a dark shadow over his soul that my spirits can quickly move in and possess.

Where once in control of his mind, I'd have him take care of his younger brother. Then when he takes the place of his father and king who will lose his mind from drink, the kingdom will be ours!"

The guards enter, bringing in a most beautiful young maiden and present her to the witch whom with reptilian gaze begins to converse.

"What is your name, fairest child?"

"Monica."

"That is a beautiful name."

"Thank you."

"Did you know you are most fortunate, Monica? For my spirits have chosen you to meet a prince on this very eve."

Monica's eyes widen with excitement. "Oh, I must go and change!"

"Now, Monica, there isn't anytime. Besides, you've no need to change for I have prepared a special potion just for you–that will take care of everything! Here, drink this."

The witch then offers her a small but deadly little bottle to drink. "He will desire you always, just the way you are from just one sip."

"Really?"

"Now would I lie to you? Although once in the castle as his bride, I might have a small favor to ask of you from time to time."

By sitting down at one of the sentry posts near the village of Orth, a lookout gives the signal to others of my approach 'til word reaches the palace.

Upon receiving notice, the witch responds, "Places everyone. Our prince approaches!"

In nervous anticipation of meeting with me, Monica drinks the witch's potion. A few moments later, some guards are found carrying her lifeless body away to a moonlit room.

The witch stretches forth her arms, transforming herself into a most beautiful queen.

I examine my situation while continuing my quest. A thought lights within my mind, *I'm just passing through–I do not want to discuss my business with anyone if asked of me.*

Next, another thought hits me, *"There's always a potential for an uprising with these Orthians."* I start to look around.

I breathe in the air and sniff to see if swords are being cast. I inhale again, only this time more deeply and let out my breath a little slower.

It is the smell of some good cooking calling to my senses, and next I'm reminded of how hungry I am, especially since my food was also in my bundle that I no longer have. The lodge was not far, though. So I consider turning while keeping my pace.

"Hey, you there!"

I turn and acknowledge this one who calls and realize I have already reached Orth. Passing by the town, it's seen my little visit has not gone unnoticed.

"Would you like a supper?"

"Why yes, I'd love some!" I have answered with my stomach, and now my thoughts are full of food. A man steps out from a crowd of observers motioning with his arm and says, "Follow me."

I follow after him, keeping up my guard–as to not do anything too hastily,

"Like accept a dinner invitation without even knowing who my host is?!"

I wasn't being very patient and did not act on a thought from a position of peace. I now see, *"I acted out of sheer hunger.*

Could this be the Great One giving a warning, or is this just a poor choice distracting me from my original purpose? A delay, so-to-speak, along the way?"

We arrive at a large stone palace towards the center of the village. *"Hey, wait a minute. I recognize this place to be Shacha's, the king of Orth. It may be a trap!"* The villager bids me to enter.

"If I refuse now he may get suspicious. Well, I've come this far, might as well see what this is all about."

Inside, I find a roomy hall with benches scattered about. It is a sort of waiting area. Then some light catches my eye from the East wing and I wander over to have a look.

"Welcome, stranger. Come in and make yourself at home."

I hesitate for what next to do. For taken in by this woman's beauty and charm upon connecting with her voice, I just freeze.

"Don't be shy now. I can assure you it is perfectly all right. I'm Queen Isabella, and it is the king's custom that any travelers who pass at meal time are invited to come dine with us."

The king is sitting across from me at the head of a long stone table taking large bites from a leg of lamb.

"I thank you very much for inviting me, your majesty, but I really should be getting on."

The queen continues to be persuasive, "Nonsense, not another word, come and sit. You must tell of where you're from and what brings you to our village, as this entertains us."

Somehow, I am moved from standing my ground. "If it pleases, your majesties, I prefer to just sit over here."

I sit down opposite the king, keeping my hood up, being careful to eat where food has already been touched.

"Tell us, oh traveler, what causes you to pass our village?"

"It's just as you say, I am a traveler. I just wonder from one village to another doing odd jobs here and there. I like to keep on the move."

"How is it that you carry no bundle?"

"I was robbed not far from here. A thief held a knife to my throat."

"How terrible! Was there anything of great value?"

"My map was important to me." The queen rings a bell resting on the table. It calls for a servant who quickly enters, "Go to the records room and bring an extra copy of the map of this region at once."

"Oh, you don't have to do that..."

"I insist!"

"Well, that'll save me some time." My thought is now, *"I won't have to go all the way to the lodge."*

There are other people sitting around the table and the atmosphere is pleasant.

The king's leg of lamb is down to the bone. My new map has been handed me. Quickly, I tuck it away in a large pocket within my robe.

"If I'd not been so anxious about leaving the castle, this is where I probably would've kept it in the first place..."

Sufficiently warming my cushion, I'm ready to take leave when a servant girl enters and whispers something in the queen's ear. She suddenly bursts out crying and turns to the king who goes to her. While they comfort each other, he begins to cry as well. Such kind people. *"They've been so nice,"* has consumed my thoughts.

"What has happened?" I enquire. "Perhaps there is something I can do to help."

"Our daughter has just died of a high fever."

"Oh, Queen Isabella. I'm so sorry. Is there anything I can do?"

"Not unless you were a prince?"

I listen further as my guard goes up.

"As remedy, a healer has left a potion for just such an emergency. We are to pour it in her mouth, have the first born son of a king kiss her, and she will come back to life. Alas, her only brother, Prince Argile, was slain in battle."

"It was as though a knife went right through me. For it was I who killed her brother in open combat, even though I don't recall King Shacha having a daughter—a thought of divine justice suddenly grabs hold of my heart."

"Take me to her!"

"Are you a prince?"

"Perhaps in my very distant ancestry, there was someone of my family who was a very great king. After all, as history teaches, are we not all fallen from our royal worth?"

"I will take you to her!"

I follow the queen from the dining area past the benches towards the west wing.

My thoughts are filled with *"'duty, honor, and truth.'*

It is the truth to love. If my kiss can bring her back to life, even if it means the risk of revealing myself to the Orthian's, then I will do it."

I enter the room where her daughter lay motionless on a table glistening in the moonlight. Its rays dance about her body through an open window. It is revealed that her beauty exceeds even that of the queen's. I approach and stand by her side.

Strangely, my thoughts are abruptly invaded with the two servants I caught embraced in a long kiss.

I start to draw near. Next, being pulled out of my senses, I enter into a trance. A tingling sensation starts to move throughout my body and I'm powerless to stop.

"Pour this potion into her mouth." The queen hands me a small bottle that I quickly open and pour into their daughter's mouth.

I'm leaning directly over her lips in the moonlight when another thought suddenly returns, bringing me to light: *You should not practice what you do not understand!*

The bottle slips from my hand landing on the stone floor with a crash. Quickly I am brought to my senses.

I look to the queen. "I'm sorry, I cannot help. I must go now."

I turn and take leave, leaving the queen, the palace, and then their village behind.

King Shacha approaches the witch, whom with a puff of black smoke turns back into her original form right before his eyes. "Why did we not force him to kiss her?"

"For a spell to work, it must be of a freewill. Otherwise, it would come back upon the one who forces. As using their own will, replacing their victims, causes great disaster. It is only for me to manipulate, then the choice is always theirs…

It is a pity our prince has to die within his soul, I rather liked hating him."

"Perhaps it is the challenge of how you're going to spell him you really love" asserts the king.

"I speak for myself, thank you. Besides, his fate has already been planned out by my special map given him, the one took of his own freewill."

"How so?"

"There's 'The Valley of the Dragon.' A deadly shortcut he'll want to take to save a half-a-days journey. This should finish him off permanently!"

"You have my interest. What is to happen?"

The witch continues. "Its valley has a spiritual flow, much like that of a whirlpool at its edge. And as he draws near, thoughts from a dragon will start to invade his mind..."

"This sounds glorious!"

"...Attacks will come upon his soul. When he uses the will of self to fight that which is of a spiritual nature, the faster he will travel towards its mouth."

"He doth not have a chance!"

"The closer Prince Liam gets, the more darkened his thoughts will become. 'Til finally, within a whirlwind, he'll be unable to understand the reasoning behind his choices. He will battle unto where he'll be drawn further into its current where he'll next beat himself up from the condemnation of his now-dragon thoughts. This will drive him mad."

"I cannot hear anymore!" the king uneasily exclaims.

"You cannot even hear of the torments of 'our prince?' What kind of soldier are you? You wanted to hear, now share in the reality of his doom!"

The witch disrespectfully continues in stride, "When our prince fights to maintain his concentration using the strength of man's wisdom, from self- will of honor, the dragon will grow even stronger.

It shall be seen by his self-righteous attitude how easily he will be overpowered, as my crystal ball reveals all."

Woven to grow accustomed to the witches thoughts of deep evil, King Shacha listens even more intently than before. Now wrapped within her pattern his thoughts become like hers.

"Finally, he will succumb to fighting fears that will grow larger than himself 'til he becomes completely overwhelmed.

Once in a state of mental exhaustion having lost his mind, he will be unable to make decisions for himself. Thus, he will be eaten by the dragon at the center of the valley.

Next, after Prince Liam has been swallowed away from his moments of existence, my occasion shall occur as the dragon will be transformed into a false version of our prince, who then will do my biding. Overwhelmed, his moments shall be mine. He shall be completely unaware of what is happening until it is too late."

"This has to work! It sounds too beautiful to fail!"

Sharing in the very same pattern of thought, the two delve in their adjoining focus. They sing in the glory of a like-minded harmonious laugh of evil, "Ah, ha, ha, hah, ha!"

IV

The moon hangs high in the sky. I'm walking at a good and even pace towards the hunting lodge when all at once, a thought comes to me.

I come out of trance, which held my mind back at Orth. Realizing I have lost my bearing, by a smell in the air, it becomes known that the Great Bog may be near. Next, I remember the map given me by the queen.

Taking advantage of the moonlight, I stop and retrieve my source of direction from inside my robe.

But haven't I been traveling the wrong direction?

"Funny, this map has different trail markings than I noticed on the other."

I figure it must be a more recent version–and am glad to see some trails I hadn't seen before–especially this one that is rather near. It shall save me at least a few hours of travel, as I'll not have to go to the lodge.

This too will keep me from a lot of backtracking and a return to Orth, as I did lose my bearing when I left their town.

I never was very much one for protocol. Besides, it rather drained me to put up with all that charm which seemed to ooze from that queen. She did leave a rather bad taste in my mouth.

Walking west for another half hour or so. I come out of the woods of Bilatz, and am met by the smell of the Great Bog again, which is swept by a wind from the bay. I realize I must be passing near the fields of Nortica. Coming to a place where the road forks, a choice is set before me. *"Do I turn off or continue on?'*

It is here I look upon a tree and find my trail to be marked by an old wooden sign hanging on a rusty nail upon its trunk. It reads, "This way to the Valley of the Dragon."

"The name rings a bell but I can't quite place it. Perhaps I will see something of the landscape along the way that will remind me of this place. Anyway, the Great One must be with me, for look at what great time I make. Why down this path, according to the map, another half-days travel will be saved.'

On the approach, I notice a few hills quickly turn to rocky crags and open into a pass within a narrow canyon. Its walls are so high, rays are blocked from the moon's light, kept from entering its depths.

I notice that beyond this point around two-hundred yards or so, there is more light again. I check my map one last time and am certain that this is the way to go.

In the canyon it is very dark, I can barely see my hand in front of my face. I stumble about a bit and am certain if I had worn my sandals instead of my boots, my feet would be bleeding by now. My thoughts next tell me how clever I am, *"Agreeing with them, thoughts of the Great One become distant."*

Now full of self-confidence, *"Still priding myself on what good time I make,"* I become anxious and pick up the pace.

Carelessly, I stop watching my steps about halfway through this ravine. The moonlight looks so close from the other side. *"Gotta hurry for the kingdom is at stake."*

Suddenly, I'm seeing stars and think it rather strange, but from the pain on my head and face and the burning on my hands and arms, I realize I have tripped on some rocks. I've had a fall.

"Now look at what you've gone ahead and done. You should have been more careful!"

Anything broken? Maybe I should wait 'til sunrise, catch some sleep and rest my wounds. I splash some water from one of my skins to clean my scrapes. Then, as I settle down for some sleep, more thoughts come to trouble me.

"Look at you—lying here. How can you rest when things are left unsettled at the castle? How can you stop and waste a single moment while your family suffers so? They need you to go on right now!

Have you pain? You've been in pain before. What would happen if you overslept? You've got to keep moving!"

As I find myself in agreement with these thoughts, I rise up and start to journey onward. Finding the way out of the canyon, my scrapes feel the sting of the open air. *"I must press on for the sake of my family. I know I can do this!"*

I stop to check that I did not lose my map and take a quick drink of water.

"If only I hadn't fallen! I can't believe I was so stupid as to be so reckless, and now I'm wasting time to stop and have a conversation with myself."

"Must keep moving!" I press on ahead with a mind full of thoughts in the presence of much darkness that surrounds. Relentlessly, they do not let up.

It seems strange, but the more I strive to do what is right, the more drained I get. Now, possessed by obsessive thoughts, I'm led to believe that I'm not *man* enough to finish my task.

I suddenly stop about halfway through the open valley and drop to my knees. My head feels like it's going to explode. All starts to spin round me and now, I'm left in a sea of total confusion.

Quickly, I try and retrace my steps for sanities sake: When I first entered the valley, I was comfortable with the pace I walked, the thought of giving up hadn't even entered my mind. Though now, my mind is all but gone. It hurts to even look at my thoughts anymore.

Why—what's left of them have become sword, beating me down into fragments of what reality used to be.

I resist, and when I do, the blows come more often 'til gradually worn within my soul.

I have lost my faith-filled shield, wherein lie the grace I need to face them. Lost without protection and defenseless, fear overcomes me in waves.

Now, becoming beaten into submission, my words are a continual pounding flow wherein the heat of their friction, hope melts away to leave a cold heart.

"What's that? What are those great billowing sounds I'm hearing?"

There are images in my mind from a fear I have, but are they of thought, or in actuality something I can fight myself?

I feel caught in its whirlpool, and the more I fight its pull, by my shocked into strength, the weaker I get. Faster and faster I slide into the movements of its swirl.

Now driven by a current, compulsively not of my own, I'm being sucked right down towards, "I can see it looming in the darkness within shadows of dizziness—It is a dragon that is causing me my pain!"

Beckoning for me to come to it, how can I resist its ploy? As its seduction offers to put me out of my miseries, even though I see its huge hideous looking teeth—

I am caught in a nightmare, only I do not awake, but by some merciful act of kindness, which leaves me stilled, I can admit that I am lost. In the midst of my turbulence, there is now a ray of light the size of a pinhole wherein some thoughts are brought to remembrance. I cry out from frustrations towards an answer, "Deliver me from the darkness of this pit!"

A rumbling sound is heard. It is the sound of an empty belly looking to be filled.

"Oh, Great One. I am afraid!"

Then there is more light. Only now, I recognize its brilliance. The sword of the Great One's trust has again placed His shield in hand. Flowing as a beacon of hope, His Spirit next enters to cover my mind.

"The mind will be kept at perfect peace whose mind is stayed on Thee."

My stance becomes shod in the ground as I stand immovable.

Stress melts away like wax, and here I recognize His voice from youth.

"With man nothing is possible, but with Me all things are possible."

Pressures miraculously lift as my sight of truth is reassured. Held together like a belt wrapped around my waist, His presence of peace has found me. "Oh, Great One. I've been such a fool!"

"It is good you know your wisdom is that of a fool. For now, I can awaken My Spirit within you and make you wise. Watch, see Me defeat this dragon as you have grown to fulfill the vision of this moment that allows Me to cut it down. My covering of protection, righteous in nature, will prevail. I will keep back its thoughts. Only trust, and this dragon shall not re-enter your heart!

Focus on loving 'The Truth,' as My gift of grace will carry you. Then *light* faster than lightning will defeat its darkness from inside your soul.

Otherwise, this scaly monster shall draw strength from your strength and will break our established pattern by overpowering our bond.

No matter what thoughts you get, do not fight them in your strength. Instead, look to the enjoyment of knowing Me. Trust in the substance of things hoped for and the evidence of things not seen. Your confidence must rely upon My goodness before I can bear you up."

"Oh Lord, let Your Spirit flow through me to defeat this dragon then!"

"It's okay to know that your opponent is there, but be confident in 'My Light' and you shall see this beast swallowed away from your path. Its fears out-shined by My affections. This is the path that will guide you through.

Now, when the dark thoughts come, keep your eyes upon our bond and do not resist. Only trust Me, and when the dragon speaks, do what it tells you to do. Recognize your pain and remember to be honest 'til I alone am kept in sight. This is where in the midst of love, you will be restrained from the pride of life."

"Yes, my Lord! I will follow this terrible dragon's lead looking towards you as your love calls me to go deeper 'til it be defeated."

While I walk as if in a trance, my mind becomes quickened to The Faster High King's Glory Light and I humbly take His hand. I now see Vine through leaf of circumstance and this becomes my door. Love of Great One now grows strong. Vision beholds sight.

It is in Your joy of heart that I'm discovered. Strength to strength I am upheld. There is now focus, abundance has my life..

A short time later, I find myself charmed while standing in front of a shrunken and innocent looking serpent. The Lord's power has put a leash on it, now having legs about the size of my fingers.

The Great One tells me to kill it by stepping on its head, but somehow I become amused. For within my pride, I instead pick it up to get a closer look.

Suddenly, I hear a thought speaking to my mind that tells me to swallow it.

The Great One in His mercy breaks this thought with His love, telling me to drop and crush it. I recognize the sound of His voice from the truth of His concerns. However, when I go to drop the dragon, it bites into my hand and tries to crawl inside. "Ouch!"

I manage to shake it off, but before I can kill it, it grows in-size to that of a cat.

Again the Great One speaks to my mind. He tells me not to kill it in anger or I will inherit its darkness and turn into a dragon myself. Now, I see what I must do.

"Lord, take my anger from me that it may be destroyed. I give it to You!"

"Why are you angry?"

"Because I got bit."

"And why did you get bit?"

"Because I didn't follow Your instructions. I'm now sorry that I did not. Although if You help me, whether I live or die, my Lord, Your salvation shall be known. For You save those who trust in Your Holiness to make them Holy by gift of grace through faith.

Even now a helmet fits within the vision I have. Where under Your authority an open heaven flows within my mind, bringing me back to Your path. I see it will be by actions that hold Your words in place. You always bring trust, delivering while bowed in the humility of holiness!"

The Spirit of peace next enters my storm that had me overshadowed. Again the dragon is driven back, shrunk down to the size of a small snake once more. It has been given to me, and walking over, I tread upon its darkened head as it meets with the heel of my boot.

There is a loud crunching sound which sparks reality. Deeply it takes root as gratitude now floods my soul. *"I know that the Great One has truly delivered this serpent into my hand. Meeting with its end, I've found an even newer and deeper love with the Great One than before."*

Exhausted, I almost faint 'til collapsing to the ground. The last thing I remember, as I'm about to close my eyes, is the blood on my hand. *"Why, it is evaporating into thin air!"* The puncture closes from the dragon's bite with scrapes disappearing as well.

Suddenly, quickened from a trance, my vision becomes clear. Curiously enough, I am found refreshed. Even at peace.

I sit up and start to rub the sleep from my eyes, but I am wide awake. Had I been dreaming? I notice the dead dragon and realize apparently not.

I sense my strength return. I rise to my feet and am met with the first rays of sunlight. A new day has dawned.

I spy out some large stones and commence to bring them over to where the dragon lay slain. After laying them on top of it before the Lord, I kneel and share my gratitude.

"Oh Great One, I thank You as this victory belongs to You. Now that all has gone well in battle, I know You are with me.

I have discovered Your passion of fire once more. You burn intimately inside, increasing in measure, and this I cherishingly adore. Again, my love is even deeper than before, known within my blood as Your new zeal finds me satisfied."

Taking leave of this place, I notice that there is something different about the valley. A change has taken place. The plants, the trees, the grass. Why even the rocks cry out in adoration towards 'The Great One.' I notice my thoughts have grown sharper, clearer, and more sensitive to my surroundings than before.

It is not just the valley for my steps are that of a gentler nature. With this new vision, I realize a change has taken place from within, one that I had nothing to do with.

I've just come to an awareness that I've been taking my breaths for granted as they are a gift from You, oh Great One.

I'm starting to really feel my royal worth, but not just that of a prince. More like of a king.

I take one last look back at the altar where my Love has just met me, knowing that He shall guard my heart from all that is evil.

My path takes on a different meaning as my footsteps now have joy. Although I take leave, I don't know if this place will ever leave my mind. "I'll not soon forget you my Great One," and again I continue on my way.

V

Recoiling into her thoughts of darkness, the witch is left with a gaze. Prince Liam is seen in her crystal ball as she looks on in a deep blank stare.

The king of Orth then barks out the question, "What do we do now?" The woman of schemes cracks an evil smile, "Be patient!"

Back at the castle, Edward is guiding father with guards through secret passage ways.

Finally they arrive at an open area that adjoins most of the other adjacent passages.

"If Liam doth not turn up here father, he has left the castle. For this is the last place I know."

"Left the castle, has he?"

"Father, why have you come looking for Liam with guard? What is going on?"

"Liam is on the run because he's tried to harm the queen..."

"Not possible!"

"He is on the run, and do not say anything to your mother as she has not yet remembered–it might even upset her further."

Grieved by the whole affair, my brother finds his way to the courtyard and sits by the frog pond. He rests upon a stone bench.

After a few reflective moments of looking at the frogs, he feels his emotions rise within. Noticing their movements while meditating upon the pond, he realizes they're in different stages of development, too. "Hey, you frogs aren't really created so different. You go through changes just like we do."

"Croak! Croak!"

Edward has a few more thoughts, "Liam and I have shared so many times together. How will I go on without him?

Yet, he's been so distant lately–I've got to find out from him what's going on. However, knowing him, not staying to look after mother, he'd probably be cross.

Perhaps I can find out from her. Although, Liam will most likely be back in a few days. Father is right, she should not be upset any further.

Wait a minute! Maybe the healer will know what to do. At least it's a possibility. Besides, I can talk to him about how disjointed the family has been lately, it'll be better than pining away here hour after hour. Perhaps he can give me ideas to bring light and resolve this situation. I will go to him."

The healer and servant girl are diligently at prayer on behalf of our queen. Edward enters the room, they look up and acknowledge my brother upon arrival and he quickly tells the physician of his plight, "So whatever shall I do? I know not what to decide."

"I can tell no man what to do, but as for myself in such a matter, I would seek out the Great One for answers. For this is where the true power really lies."

"What is your counsel, though? Are you not older and wiser? You see more of the valley of life than I do. You've been further up the mountain than I."

"If I were to tell you what to do, it would not help your climb up the mountain. Yet, if you love the truth more than you love yourself, you will have light to seek the Great One's favor on what path you're to choose on your climb."

My brother responds lowering his chin to his chest. After a pause, he raises his eyes towards heaven. "I have heard what you have said. I will go and seek out the Great One. Perhaps it is time for me to get better acquainted with him firsthand."

"That is a very good choice."

While following the trail on my map, I next encounter a small village and pigs are scrambling everywhere.

I pass a group of huts with thatched roofs. They have small vegetable gardens interwoven between them on my right and there is a watering hole on my left. More huts are on either side of the road along the way.

At about midway through the village, I start to wonder where all the people are.

All at once, I feel a tugging at the bottom of my robe. I look down to see a young girl around age seven with the bluest of eyes. She catches my attention while looking up at me and asks, "Are you a priest?"

"Well, what is your name?"

"Danielle," she replies while continuing to tug on my robe. Then dropping to her knees she tries to make out my face from beneath the hood. Then she asks again, "Are you a priest?"

"Hmmm! Sort of."

"My mama is going to die if you don't come!"

Remembering what the Great One has just done for me in the 'Valley of Dragon,' I answer saying, "Well, let's have a look."

Led by the hand, Danielle takes me up a side path and then back to her hut.

I know nothing of healing except that sometimes I would take potion when sick and somehow get better.

I enter her hut and see her mother lay shivering on a bed woven from dry grass set within a wooden frame. Although there is a blanket over her, even in this heat, she still shivers. I kneel by the side of her bed and wait 'til I am certain there is nothing I can do but call upon The Great One.

I notice that Danielle's tear-filled eyes are fixed upon me. Then the few that escape begin to melt the rest of my heart. "What would you have me to do, Danielle?"

"Lay your hands on her and pray."

I slowly extend my arms as some dark thoughts start to come, *"You'll probably get her fever and die."–"You lied to her. You are not a priest, the Lord will not hear your request."*

As I rest both my hands on her feverish forehead, I proclaim, "Get back, you dragon!" Next, remembering how I was healed from the bite of the serpent along with my scrapes, I am filled with compassion.

Now my love flows from within the truth of His truth. Looking unto the deep from beyond above, I then cry out, "In the Name of the Great One who has healed me, be well!"

I feel her mother's forehead grow suddenly cool. Then eyes open as her turning body sits up to face us.

Danielle and I hug each other warmly.

I next hear her mother speak from her concerns, "Danielle, who is this man you've brought into our home?"

"He is a priest and he has healed you!"

Her mother continues to look on, "Oh, I thank you for your kindness."

"Praise be to our Great One, for it is he who has healed you. Now how is it that everyone has left the village and only you two remain?"

"A witch came and claimed this village for herself, saying, "We needed to pay her tribute or all would die. Because I believed the Great One to be greater than her spells, I alone remained with my daughter."

"I see you have great faith to have remained…"

"And yours must be even greater—For you have been used by His hand."

Danielle's mother then invites me to have a meal with them.

I tell them how "I must keep moving because I am pressed for time." However, she doth convince me to take some fresh fruits and vegetables along.

She packs them in a pouch-like bag with a thick drawstring and padding at its center; this is where it rests upon my neck.

The string reaches over my head and hangs by my side just under one of the waterskins which are crossed over my shoulders.

They walk me back to the main road, and after a big hug from Danielle, she waves goodbye as I part in peace.

As I leave the village behind, Danielle's love remains. I must say, *"Just as the dragon was conquered, a part of me was conquered from my brief encounter with the villagers.*

There is now a place within my soul where my love flows with even greater freedom than before.

All is told by a deep abiding joy that sets me aglow 'til at last I'm met with a smile upon my face."

I know I am being changed, crafted into being gentler by the Great One. I shall contain His Spirit and always be fulfilled within His purpose in my life. At last, I am sure of it.

Yet, all the pieces have not quite come together. There's a need to know more. Indeed, *"I now go to the priests with a greater understanding of what I am to look for when I reach them."*

The village fades into the background, and according to the map, the Mountains of Zantee lay just after the Tall Hills, which I happen to be three quarters of the way through.

Let me see, the monastery lies pretty much somewhere straight ahead. But how far really?

I take a drink which finishes off one of the skins of water. The thought then comes, *"I should have filled it at the village."*

Hmmm! *"Got sidetracked by the blessing of that lovely little girl and breaking the spell of that witch. I don't remember any signs on the map for water either. I guess it's up to You now, oh 'Great One,'"*

I pray in further reflection, *"Have mercy on me the way you did for Danielle and her mother."* I decide not to go back to the village for water. Too far. *"It's just not in me to do it! You slayed the dragon. You broke the fever, and now I'm ready for you to be my confidence over water as well. I'll not turn back!'"* Heatwaves start to rise from the ground. This makes travel almost unbearable. *"Has impatience gotten the better of me?"*

Yet, I choose to listen to more encouraging thoughts when I discover how quickly the water is going. Seeing the pass through the mountains of Zantee ahead, I seek direction from the Great One.

"Yes, if I were to conserve my strength by resting 'til the heat of the day wore on, I would use less water and be able to travel faster on through the night as the moon be full this eve, too. That's a wonderful idea, my Great One"

I walk a little while longer before coming to a suitable spot: plenty of shade, soft grass, and no sign of poisonous bugs or serpents. I am thankful to the Great One for providing such a spot and make camp.

After resting, I awake to long shadows across the trail when my body tells me how hungry I am. Then opening the pouch the villager's gave me, I discover the name 'Samantha' embroidered on it. This must have been Danielle's mother's name. My heart sings out to the Great One for providing for me. Thoroughly, I enjoy a meal of fresh fruits and vegetables, this gives me much needed strength before moving on.

Meanwhile, back at the castle, "...Oh Great One, watch out for my dear brother Liam. Grant him safe passage on his journey wherever he may be."

Edward, who has been praying in his room, has lost track of time as he lays before the Great One. Rising to a kneeling position, he notices that the sun has already set. Feeling at peace, my brother stands to his feet. Then lighting a candle, Edward notices that he's been deeply filled. He next starts to laugh and dance in pleasant joyous circles, while smiling on the inside.

Coming to a stop, he suddenly shouts out, "I have been with the Great One!"

There is one thought now on his mind, "I am going to wait to see how things unfold–

As peace means for me to stay, here is where I'm going to stay.

Now, I am certain to trust that all will go well. I am mindful to remember all time belongs to You, oh Great One."

My brother leaves his room, and while passing the courtyard, voices are heard. He next overhears one of two scouts talking with father as they walk.

Anticipating news of myself, Edward eavesdrops while trying to go unnoticed. He conceals himself in the shadows behind a nearby colonnade and listens, "Sire, while making my usual rounds, I came upon three of the chief kings riding together. I quickly took cover and made like I was checking my horse's leg in case they did see me as to not arouse their suspicions."

"Well, what did they say?"

"I could only tell by the expressions on their faces that they were pleased about something. They then rode off towards Orth."

"Orth. Hmmm! If the tribes were to hold council without a representative from Calington, it would be a direct violation of our treaty. On the morrow, you will find a place where you can see everyone coming out of and going into Orth - without being seen of course. Take provisions, you may be there a few days before I send relief. We must find out what is happening!"

"Yeah, sire!" The scout takes leave.

King Henry starts to suddenly shake while drawing his arms to his chest. He next steadies himself.

After regaining his composure, he looks towards his other scout, "You will have to come with me, as my golden goblet beckons."

Edward steps out into the court from alongside the colonnade beneath the balcony where he'd been hiding.

Approaching as if passing by, he next overhears the scout who gives report while walking with the king, "Nothing to report about Prince Liam yet, sire. I am sorry."

"I want you to journey further out on the morrow. This time bring out the guard, I want him found...

Wait! I believe I know where he may be."

After overhearing father, Edward keeps walking while regaining his composure. Once alone, he lights a candle in his room and returns to prayer.

VI

The sun hangs high in the sky, night has faded hours ago. It is to my misfortune, this day proves to be even hotter than the one before. My steps keep falling into place as though I'm being carried. My strength has all but failed.

Is my mind playing tricks on me? Do I see a building complex beyond heat waves rising from the ground ahead?

Turning off the trail, slowly they appear before me. I see two large wooden doors as I draw near. One of the doors has a large polished brass knocker. It comes into focus within its grain at center, just above the handles.

Having arrived at what I presume to be the monastery, I reach out with the remainder of my strength and grasp hold. Again and again I knock–I thirst, as I continue to hang on to the ring of the knocker. Having run out of water, walking all night into the heat of the midday sun my mind is all but gone.

"Great One, I can hold on no longer. Hear me, into Thy hands do I commit my trust."

Awakening sometime later, I feel a cool damp cloth upon my forehead. Slowly, my sight returns to focus, and looking around, I discover myself to be in a large room full of beds.

Next, I remember the sound of the bolt while holding onto the ring of the brass knocker; must have passed out after that.

Maybe returning to the village for water was the better plan after all. "The castle!" I go to sit up, and am quick to realize how drained I am, then slump back down into bed.

"Oh, it's good to see you're with us."

I turn my head and notice a robust man of stature is sitting on the other side of me.

"How long have I been sleeping for?"

"Just a day."

"A whole day? I have to get up," but when I go to do so, my strength again leaves me.

"Hey, easy there. It's all in the Lord's timing, you know!"

I look at the serenity on his face and see this priest has just meant what was said.

"My name is Jerome. Here, take a drink of water."

He hands me a drink from a ladle drawn from a small wooden bucket. I have to steady it with both my hands to keep from spilling at first, but after a few more tries I am able to master it.

"Good, I'm glad you're able to do that on your own." He next rings out a sponge filled with water before placing it in a small bowl next to my bed. He looks over, "We thought we'd drown you any other way, but you needed water."

"Please, I am looking for Louis Cardier and Andre Solan. Are they here?"

"They are in prayer right now."

"Glorious! I am probably one of the ones they pray for—it's the only way I could have made it through 'The Valley of the Dragon.'"

"I was taught that that place was only a myth."

"Well, the same map that brought me here led me past there as well. Here, have a look."

With a bit of effort, I take out the map from the inside pocket of my robe and hand it to him, "See for yourself."

I watch intently as Jerome studies the map.

"Hmmm! According to these markings this is a spiritual map with a hex on it. You were to have met with your end 'here' in this valley."

Pointing to the location of 'Dragon Valley,' Jerome looks to me and asks straight way, "What was the color of this line where it is now green?"

"That's funny, I could have sworn it was red."

"This map has the markings of a blood curse upon it and must be destroyed."

"But on the way here on one of its trails, the Great One used me to heal someone under a witch's enchantment after slaying a dragon. Besides, it was presented to me by the Queen of Orth personally!"

"The Great One doth work all things for good by those who love Him. This much is true—but on the other hand there is no Queen of Orth.

You have been deceived." He hands back my map.

A sudden look of surprise overtakes my eyes as Jerome continues, "According to the move of the Spirit who gives visions, there is a powerful witch that has undergone the sleep of doom…"

"What's that?"

"A sleep where the soul has no light so that evil itself may have its way with it at will. The one who gave you this map could've been that very same, darkened, witch. If not for the grace of the Great One, you would have met with certain death."

"Gulp!"

Extending forth the map, I bid for him to take it, "If you please, I've had enough happen to me already."

Jerome takes the map and folds it under his arm. "How will you destroy it?"

"By the same way the witch will be destroyed–with eternal fire!"

"What's that?"

"The Great One has brought you to us. He is the One who will draw you unto himself. You will learn when the time is right."

"Well said, Jerome."

"Louis!... Andre!"

Louis, "You were right Prince Liam, we were praying for you."

"This is Prince Liam I've been speaking with."

Jerome bows his head, "Your majesty," but then raises it before looking at me again. He next lets out what is upon his heart, "We've all been praying for you–and your family–and now you're here."

"I see you treat all men with a royal worth at this place. My many thanks to you, Jerome, for both your kindness and much needed prayers.

Now, Louis, Andre, come over by my side. I've many questions to ask of you."

I next hear Louis, "Liam, I believe it would be wise for you to get some rest."

Followed by Andre, "You'll have strength on the morrow, we can talk then."

They are aglow with the righteous judgment of love from prayer, but I let impatience get the better of me.

"Louis, you can't be serious. Why it's practically the middle of the day.

Andre, tell him otherwise!"

"Your majesty, what good is an answer that will only drain you of your strength right now when you can rest? I too believe that your refreshed thoughts will be better on the morrow."

After a brief ponder, I see the wisdom in what was just said and am humbled by it.

"I've heard you well, Andre. All right then. By the Great One's might, I will see you on the morrow–Oh, what is to happen? I mean, where will I to meet with you and Louis?"

"After breakfast, Jerome will bring you to us. We've lessons for you if you're willing to learn a thing or two."

I quickly rest my head on my pillow and stretch out on the bed. "You know, Andre, I believe he's finally ready to grow."

"I see it too. What a change has come over him."

Louis says reassuringly, "See how he now shares in our quest. His hunger most definitely has a love for the truth."

"I wonder if he knows he is at the verge of the greatest adventure of all..."

"By the Great One's timing, I believe he is ready to join us."

I share in Andre's and Louis's excitement, but sleep has the better of me. I doze off with a thirst for the truth, knowing its the *desire* I really seek.

Later on at eve, I am awakened from the soundness of my sleep; there are the sounds of many voices. I listen as my eyes crack open to see priests everywhere. Why, it is their prayers that I am hearing.

Filling the beds about me, they call upon the Great One as a closer friend than known. Their prayers are heard in bits and pieces.

Intrigued, I listen further. My senses are coming in tune while lying in bed—my focus is becoming centered.

One priest prays: "Oh, my gentle Great One—lover of my soul, I thank You for Your strength that has met me throughout the gift of another day." More prayer is heard: "Thank You for the love of my many brothers." Another priest prays: "Grant that Queen Mary will walk again. Bring healing to her back and comfort her in her time of need." Then again: "Fill my heart, Lord. Let it ever be true."

And finally: "Oh Lord, my heart is broken over my sister's husband. I haven't the strength to carry on—Be my strength that I may pray for her family. I know that You not only have the power to strengthen, but change their situation, too."

I drink in their faith like a thirsty plant, as their own love for the truth further encourages me.

After listening for awhile–I too find myself giving thanks to the Great One: "Hold my future and carry me through what I must face to fulfill Your plan" surfaces within my soul, loosened by their prayers before turning to quiet heartfelt praise and all else that follows. My words become my thoughts, which rests upon His Peace, and again I am brought back to sleep.

After what I must admit, a rather impatient breakfast, I walk with Jerome to meet the others.

The weather is fair. Louis and Andre, along with a whole host of priests, are working in a very large vegetable garden. It strikes me immediately, as they work the field, just how content they all look.

Some of the gardeners back at the castle would curse the very ground they walked on. I am happy to be amongst men who have purpose in their work.

My focus then shifts, coming in tune with a hardy greeting, "Good morn, Brother Louis, Brother Andre. Here is your pupil."

Jerome bows his head, as he's met by a messenger who whispers something to him.

"Our Monsignor wishes to see me, Liam. I'll see you later, your majesty." He then takes leave rather quickly.

All of a sudden, it has grown very quiet and I hear the word *prophecy* whispered amongst the other priests.

Louis holds up his hand, saying, "Now, now. We all have our parts to play." Rather cheerfully they then return to their work.

"What do they mean by *prophecy*?" I inquire.

"Today's lesson is in the garden, everything else will come in its time, Liam."

"Very well then, Louis. What am I to learn?"

"Look around, tell me what you see."

"I see a very large garden filled with brethren that are working in our interest."

"Good! That is a part of the big picture. Now, what are the building stones that bring such an event to pass?"

My mind fluctuates, "My vision speaks of lots of things."

"Now focus in on one of them—and take your time before you speak."

"Well, without the garden, we would not be here."

"And why not?"

I pause and start to reason in the light, *"Whatever my response, unless I humble myself with consideration and ask clarification, I see that many more questions will follow.*

Although this question was asked directly to me—this makes me want to get to the heart of the matter.

I'm impatient, but then the thought of how patient the Great One must be with me through the example of the priests comes to mind." Finally, I give answer, "I think I need more time."

"We can come back on the morrow."

"No, not that much time!"

I go over my thoughts again and find I cannot justify a position which would keep me from drawing closer to completion. I question myself, *"Is this a test?"*

Yet, I must remain who I am if I am to stay on the correct path or be kept from the fullness of the Great One's true reward.

I then conclude, *"By following the truth of this path, perhaps I am being taught through my own questioning, for only the truth is able to push away any confusion that I may have."*

Praying quietly to myself, I go over the thoughts that are in my mind, *"Oh Great One, I want to gain understanding to see the way I am to grow, as I suspect it will lead to the healing of my many hurts received within our changing kingdom. For I know in Your light, I will find what is keeping me incomplete."*

I finally answer Louis again, "Without food from a garden, we could not live well."

"And where do the plants come from?"

"The Great One provides them for us."

"How?"

"Oh, I am losing my patience! What do you want of me?"

"You see those apple trees at the end of the field? Point one out."

I look over and point to the tallest of several trees in a small grove.

"Now, could that tree have grown to be so tall if it kept getting up and walking around?"

"No."

"And why not?"

"It would lack in root to support its own weight–water–or even sunlight if it stood in the wrong place."

"This is what happens when we lose our patience–as only *still* moments go into giving us a complete picture."

I freeze in my thoughts before returning to focus. He has brought me to a place where I can fully understand which brings more life–and now I am dumbfounded by the beauty of his answer. "Oh my. When we lose our patience, we lose our order and are without structure.

Why, from what I see, when we become as a wandering tree, we cannot grow very well–if at all. For how can we, if the stages of where we begin and end are not there? I see now. When out of the moment, we lose the vision of our sight."

"What belongs to the Great One, we cannot lose."

"But I have given Him my confidence, which causes me to grow!"

"Now, He is asking for your patience as well, for this is another one of His stages of growth you've to know. Reality must come together upon our spiritual tree bit-by-bit, growing beyond ourselves to become a part of Him. Asking by prayer, this is how we find our center for a full life, wherein we must remember to draw strength from the enjoyment of truth from Him. Then containing the order of life comes within ourselves when He brings it.

You will learn. Liam. Each stage of growth fulfills a purpose playing a part in the development of our souls. It is only in the timing of the Great One we become knowledgeable of the depths of His unmerited favor wherein we know grace.

Our moments with Him grow longer while progressing in the perfection of Him. Then when understanding comes on how we're always in progression, humility next visits our vision. For in realizing we've been changed without our own doing, this is where we grow in our relationship with Him." I stand as a thirsty sponge and gladly drink in the words of Louis.

"My focus has just grown a little sharper. I now recognize, again, that the pattern of my being has been altered since last night in the light of what has just been spoken.

I am becoming more patient not by my own doing. It is the beauty of His truth that has slowed me down to where I'm now more filled with life!

Why, I've started to comprehend that in relating with the Great One, I must recognize that I am lacking. Secondly, I must rely upon Him to make me whole, it is only now that I start to know my value as seen within the sharing of the Great One's wisdom of light.·

"Louis, I'm starting to understand–if I am to learn, I've to ask Him to let His power take the place of my own."

"You know, Prince Liam, you have been growing all along but have not been aware of all of the changes that have taken place in you.

It has been most unfortunate that we were not able to instruct you because of the division at the castle. Although, as wisdom told us we were to leave, our prayers have been with you and the kingdom ever since.

We knew by faith that the Great One would cause you to grow through soil of circumstance 'til you came to us. The Great One even told us that you were here when we were in prayer, this is why we came out to you. His Spirit reveals all to them that love Him, and now you have become as a pool filled with life."

"I see–and my smiling from joy reveals what you say to be true."

"Liam, because it was revealed to you at the castle that your father's spirit has changed towards a destructive manner, you have left his rule. In this place things are different.

As here, you will find encouragement to help you grow beyond the darkness of this world which is being consumed by spirits of evil. For as the fire of light brings the enjoyment of deep reality to you. You will learn more of the Great One's desire to know you more. It shall further be revealed how to know eternal life contained, in place of the dryness of stagnant time. Now my good pupil, Andre will instruct you further."

"Wait a minute! Let me take all this in. You say the Spirit of the Great One rules over all the other spirits with the greatest of all light, and is the giver of life that all can enjoy Him when *stilled*. Hmmm, that would explain what happened in 'The Valley of the Dragon', plus, a whole lot more."

Some unexpected thoughts come bubbling up, "I've just remembered. I've had the same dream three times in a row. I must know about the deliverer..."

"All will be revealed in the timing of the Great One, Liam."

I next hear a word from my other instructor."Thank you, Louis. Those words were well spoken."

After hearing his voice, I then look towards Andre. Next, I get a look that reminds me to thank Louis, too. Now that I've tasted the Spirit behind their words, my appetite's become whet. I can tell this by how easily my own words come to my lips. "Thank you, Louis. You've prepared me to know how hungry I am. I'm now completely ready to listen to Andre."

Opening up his hand, Andre invites my attention. He tells me to watch what he is doing and then asks, "What have I just done?"

"You have planted seed into the soil."

"We start beneath the soil as such seed, 'til we receive our faith as food, which comes from the Great One. Is this understood?"

I am then reminded of how the Great One revealed himself to me. "I know His light entered my mind when battling the darkness of a dragon."

"Good. For this is the same way grace meets with us as seed, sown into the stillness of our tilled and fertile soil. All who recognize this know they need to grow into the full gift of life.

As it is known, our roots seek out the best nutrients to sustain life's substance when ready to be watered with care.

In the final outcome, thoughts are examined and guide all to make choices. We either stay in the soil or seek another path. All is discovered to aid in growth of truth in every answer within each question, blooming much like that of a plant. For breaking forth from beneath darkness contained, we too enter a new world of light, well on the way to becoming a thriving plant. Though it must not be forgotten we started out as humble seed.'"

I listen further.

"Once all the conditions have been graciously met, set in order and being faithful with little, your relationship with the Great One will grow to know Him even more. Continue to see this, then your purpose shall bring you to completion in life. You will sense He is making you whole. Trust, and you will be held trustworthy. His stable base shall build you up. Wait and see, He will make you faithful over much."

"I am starting to experience a greater measure of faith already, where all is understood from what is now known as it causes me to draw nearer to Him. This is the help I need, for I feel His fullness in the light of His love bringing me the joy of clarity!"

"Excellent, as this is the kind of plant that grows. Likened unto being supplied with joyous food, giving relief from a parched dry land. Know that safe haven is offered from spirits of the air as these dragons, just like birds of prey, would otherwise spot their next victim.

Provision is provided here, like material for hungry souls which search for truth; as they, like caterpillars, will find their way throughout creation. Where eating of its leaf and spinning thread of The Great One's substance, all becomes known as everything shall remain 'til a new pattern is formed.

Then once wrapped in the truth, a soul will emerge to show the glory of the Great One's colors in the next stage of life, like that of a butterfly in freedom."

Andre continues, "Its branch will further invite all kinds of creature and shelter them from the darkness of this parched world.

Then, as others continue to come for shade, the vine of truth shall protect and yield comfort from all the other elements.

The beauty of its budding flowers will then reveal the glory of the Great One. For it is He who has given life to the plant and everything that has touched it!

The Lord always displays what is from within. Its fragrance will then crown the atmosphere, when in bloom. Give proclamation to full given worth with further invitation or tell of what is lacking; as within the story of a dead branch that no longer thrives."

"I see, this is liken to my father being honored when given fan-fair in making public appearances."

"It can be looked at in this way, as one's presence is an announcement–Let me bring you to the next stage in which the Spirit announces itself. Looking at a busy buzzing bee, makes one mindful of its colorful skills in design.

Here, transformation of the flower's sweet pollen is transformed to nectar before honey. This food substance aids in sustaining the lives of many. Once the fragrant flowers yield to the aroma of ripe fruit, finally it is ready to complete the cycle of life."

I hear the hoes of the priests tilling the soil about me, but even this doth not break my focus.

"Those who come for shade discover eating ripe fruit 'til satisfied. Wisdom is the substance crafted by the true vine of design. Our Lord's own hand, by the essence of His word, will always hold truth where all the senses are fed.

The gift of His purpose next bears fruit inside ourselves, where feeding one another as an act of love satisfies within a circle to make us family. We started out as babes feeding from within our mother's safe and fruitful womb. Yet outside as a part of our Lord's plan, when taught direction, we find Him best to meet all needs. It must be understood that in knowing ourselves better, His glory is reflected to all else.

More seed occurs from overripe fruit–spilling over from bountiful joy. Then once no one has eaten of the truth of it, the soil again receives seed for future blessings with more of His message left behind. Others find and feed upon this new life and know His hand that crafts.

For those who are willing to trust to have His seed in the soil of an open heart, it remains waiting as the Great One has *occasion* on how He will continue the truth behind His cycle of growth.

He feeds here with words of affirming love that you too have witnessed. For by His patient-loving peace within a soul. All grow to gain further entrance in His kingdom after a life realizes it rests while filled inside it."

Now deeply moved, I am stirred yet again. "The sound of our Great One's peaceful love brings me much joy, as even more clarity comes to steady me."

"This joy must be preceded by depths of heavenly peace holding us in His garden of love, or death will take its place to dry out life within it."

"Then I will call upon Him to *still* my ways, and I'll remain within the Lord's affirming love as often as it takes to find focus upon His root."

"If you do this, death shall cease and joy will flow as 'restoration.' Rest inside this kind of peace and you shall always know of the grateful vine of gratitude. For you too will do good to remember that plants will not grow very well in soil that is not fertile.

So, you shall be made ready to focus on Him while in unceasing prayer, for only the Great One can prepare the richest soil of nutrients to produce the best life in you.

For actions and attitudes behind words tell of how we are meeting with His love to live in joy or not. Be ever mindful to watch your words and what thoughts are behind them before they come out of your mouth. For rather than light, you may invite darkness.

Be in necessity and you shall have sight of light to grow with clear perception, turn to the Great One as often as it takes then over again. For once *all* becomes familiar to you on a foundation of peace, sight will have direction. Otherwise, fumbling shall drive you around in confusion of the dark, and nothing grows here."

"This is all so wonderful. Where did you get such knowledge?"

"It is only because you have asked that I may tell you, Prince Liam. There are living pages called the *Book of Life* which came from the root of the Great One's sacrifice. By reading these pages in sequence, line upon line within the timing of our Great One, we become fertile souls laying at rest. Then by meditating upon more words within His gentle spirit, we are watered."

"But how is this possible?"

"I'll tell you, although you are consistent in your repetition, it will not put you in touch with your true self unless your behavior lines up with the melody of Spirit from the words found in the *Book of Life*."

"What if it doth not line up?"

"Those who acknowledge that there are spiritual forces which steal, are not kept in shadows as their new desire is guidance of light. Realize that life is far greater than it seems, Prince Liam!"

All at once, it rises within me and a dark thought comes out, "Just because your life is centered around the Great One, I don't have to agree if it's not my choice!"

I am surprised, *"These words have come out of my mouth."*

Andre responds with compassion by asking me a question in a soothing way, drawing me out of myself and into his confidence, "Are you all right?"

"Why do you ask?"

"Liam, would you mind if I asked? Upon what do you base your choices?"

"Me, I guess."

"Liam, I sense this is difficult for you. Would you like to stop here?"

"No, I want to go on."

"Are you sure?"

"I'm okay. Really Andre, I want to learn!"

"All right then, Liam. Where doth 'me' get thoughts to make choices?"

I am stunned and cannot answer. *"It is only now that I see I am ready for instruction."*

I look directly into Andre's eyes. So much love, his smile tells of such joy.

"I next wonder, where his first thoughts came for growth?"

"Liam, you must walk in the light while you have light from the Great One's Spirit within. Do not fear, as you will learn the *Book of Life* keeps us lit and darkness out beyond prior choice of our free wills."

"Then it is the Great One who made me to receive His thoughts? Is this where your first thoughts of Him have come as well?"

"Yes, we are all His beings."

"What is in this 'Book of Life?'"

"I can only tell you that it is the Great One's gift to us. From this time forth, if He is read everyday, you shall know Him directly by His pages, too."

"Why can't you tell me more?"

"Priests are but a stepping stone to the Spirit of the Great One's root. All else we learn from one another, while making our mistakes on the path of discovering wisdom. We all must be humble enough to know that outside of God's Spirit we are far from infallible.

Be honest and watchful as this is the set standard one need follow. For it teaches us the pattern on how being good stewards over our own souls helps others, too.

When you too can admit that you are not able on your own–You will not only be ready to hear from the 'Book,' but be ready to take Him to heart sincerely.

As you must remember, your own relationship with the Great One needs balance and order to retain what you have learned. For we are being built firmly upon Him to know the function of our path while he crafts out where we belong. In this I'm sure, you will find place for purpose when on the Great One's path, the one that we all need for a full life."

"May I read this 'Book of Life?'"

"Before you do–You must first understand that the life which will come from the Spirit of this book is not of the wisdom of man, lest the Spirit of the Book become emptied of its power."

"Prince Liam! Prince Liam!" It is Jerome who calls to me in a rather unsettling way. I look over with great respect and acknowledge as he informs me, "The Monsignor would like to see you right away."

I look over at Louis and Andre who say together, "It is always in the timing of the Great One."

VII

Although I walk with Jerome, my mind has *Book of Life* Imprinted upon it. My thoughts next tell me *"I must be patient to see how things will unfold.'*

We pass many corridors but don't say much.

As we walk, my pattern of thought reaches the reality of a door that I am kept from passing through.

"I'm frustrated by my attempts to enter in knowing it is beyond my reach, but at least I have the satisfaction of knowing it's there...'

Then brought to a marvelous light, I am at a place of assurance, *"It doth exist!'*

Now helped, I regain the joy of the moment. The Spirit lifts and carries me. *"I will endure all things, for I sense I'm on the right path from the little bit of contentment I now have...*

Why, I'm to grow like Andre's tree and then for sure I shall reach its prize. For by faith I will gain access right on through and then up into the full heights of heaven itself.'

We come to a stop in front of two large oak doors. Jerome knocks on one of them and waits for a response. "Who is there?"

"It is Jerome with Prince Liam, Monsignor."

"You may enter."

The door opens and I follow Jerome into a large study with many books. The Monsignor is seated behind a large cherry wood desk, intricate carvings are about its trim and frame.

My eyes then catch sight of a most lovely young maiden. I can tell this by her purity of heart, which shows through serene eyes. She in turn, is poised beside the desk with a lovely glow about her countenance that emanates from her soul.

His Eminence rises from his desk, and bowing slightly he says in a deep voice, "Your Majesty!"

He then turns to the young woman and says, "This is Ashley, my niece, she has asked if she could meet with you."

She lowers herself with a curtsy and responds with a soft spoken voice, "Majesty."

I help her rise by taking her hand, then the Monsignor bids that it is time for her to go. He looks back towards Jerome and myself while clearing his throat, "Won't you be seated?"

When sitting down, I see my map lying at the right-hand corner of the desk, which captures my attention momentarily.

Next, while clearing his throat again, the Monsignor continues, "Prince Liam, from what I've seen and heard about you, I must say you are most fortunate to be alive.

In fact, if it were not for the grace of the Great One, I know you'd be dead by now, for according to our prophets who have had visions concerning both you and your father..."

"What did they see?"

Suddenly, thoughts of suspicion arise, "Hey! Why did the priests leave our kingdom when we needed them most?"

"In the wisdom of the Great One, it was the only thing they could do.

Your father would no longer receive our counsel. You see, it would have created hostility between him and the church of which he is a member.

Had we stayed to counsel further, the subjects would have been drawn into a perception of a different line of reasoning, one where a possible conflict of division would have sparked an internal war!"

Jerome interjects, "Your father would've taken it personal. So in this situation we withdrew, for a season, preserving the church 'til a time the Great One would have us return. Under His supervision, knowing 'God works all things for good for those who love Him,' by faith it was time to trust Him to guide with the greater plan.

We knew that in our absence, all would be preserved within His divine timing. We then prayed to the Great One that all would be most powerfully worked out."

I take in what they say and know their counsel to be accurate.

Now that they have my trust, I ask "What did the prophets say happened to father?"

His Eminence then shares, "A drop by itself may seem harmless, but if you put enough of them together, there can be such a flood it can wash a kingdom of a mind away."

"You refer to my father's thirst for wine..."

"And the spirits that go along with it, I'm sorry to say. However, it was through prayer, the Great One gave us a vision revealing the root cause regarding this problem."

"Please tell me what it is that we may address this matter!"

"The Tribe of Orth hired a witch for dark counsel against Calington. It seems to have taken place right after the king of Orth and the other surrounding tribes gave up their land rights. Paying taxes, as tribute to Calington, after war has led to much resentment; enough for them to seek revenge.

Under the witch's advice, a spell with a blood oath during a secret meeting was cast against your father who is our beloved king.

"Strike the head and the kingdom shall fall. Dim his light, and confusion will follow."

"How do you know this to be true?"

"Every dark deed of evil is brought into the light for those who love the truth."

"Do you know what this spell is?"

"I know you're concerned for your father, but be patient with me, my prince. For it is my desire that you will learn all I know."

Upon hearing this, I lean back, take a breath, and give him my complete attention.

"I am ready, Monsignor."

His Eminence continues, "It was through Brother Joel's vision that we learned the tribes organized a plot to have disputes amongst themselves. A deception of zoning for land payments in a fair tax levy, which only our king could resolve was invented.

The witch set it all up: The tribes put together a 'Peace Feast' and invited the king who they claimed as their ruler of the lands.

He was led to believe that He needed to solve this dispute.

He was told behind their eyes of deceit there'd be a long and lasting peace, but while all this was taking place the witch had another plan."

Jerome now states the facts: "She had them prepare a special golden goblet under specific conditions. Then, as the cup was cast with coins offered to spark greed with additional incantation of melodious song, an accursed spirit was called up.

All who sang along with her would receive power from this very same spirit as it fed upon the attacks of the king's countenance.

The spells creation breached his armor of character opening his mind, and continues to afflict him. He has been victimized ever since.

Your father, in the name of protocol, never suspected that whoever drank from the spirit of this goblet would receive an unquenchable thirst for strong wine. For when presented as gift, the golden goblet quickly seized him..."

"You knew and you did nothing to stop it! Why, you're no better than the witch!"

The Monsignor defends the priesthood, "We didn't receive this vision 'til after your father had already sipped from the golden goblet. He was already deceived by its spirit that keeps him from listening to us!"

"My father never drinks. How did they convince him?"

"They treated him especially well, making him feel more important than he really was. This is what led him to complacency while in the melody of their company.

With all the matters settled so quickly, they presented our majesty 'The Golden Goblet' and proposed a toast thanking him that a war was prevented sparing many lives.

But when he politely drank with all those who had earlier chanted against him, his pride entered in and the spell was sealed."

"I don't understand why they didn't just kill him."

"Your father withheld a very high standard of honor…"

"And will again!"

"…If an enemy can discredit our king, the cause would not be as strong. By bringing disunity to the land, we'd be more vulnerable to attack."

"Poor father, Wait a minute! Is there any way we could break the spell?" Jerome gives the solution: "A person who holds a place in his heart that's been near and dear to him through affection, must bring warming love through sewing threads of light for healing.

Painting an image of our Great One's deeper reality of love sewn to truth will bear *sight* for him to have balance again, as darkness of spirit will be cast out for his mood to swing back into position. Heart and mind will return to balance as well, where eternity shall shine at his door once more.

Then his majesty, by crushing the cup beneath his foot, shall keep this dragon spirit from entering his heart again."

"This will close the door on the spell for this sorcery to remain no more?"

"Yes, and furthermore, 'If you are willing, Prince Liam, you must get by the defenses of this evil spirit and gain access to your father's mind. Knowing what you've actually experienced of the Great One's words of rational love, this shall be your armor. This is where you will discover a breach beneath all other spirits. This is how they will be cut off.

Once uprooted from your father, he will be held in brilliance; a position of boundary of honor by the Great One's Angel shall restore him again.'"

"Why not just tell my father about this spell, won't this break it?"

"The cup has become his only source of comfort, wherefore he would deny the truth and have nothing more to do with you as the lie of this deception has completely possessed His mind.

You have the power to open his heart to trust. It is here, with patience, you shall go beyond forcing and respectfully gain access to flush out his soul. What be hid beneath his footing, dark spirited roots, will then burn away as they lose their deception of control. They will be defeated by pressing into love in times of uneasiness, as this is what eternal light doth do.

Liam, in this light, you shall cause him remembrance of your love, but it will only be a start. For our Great One has a timing where He will establish His peace as base, 'til all be set upon loving grace.

For now, prayers will prevent further damage from the advancement of this enemy while building to restore your father to life. Acts of true love with compassion must be taken or he will slip away into the abyss due to a further lack of light. So be mindful to pray, Liam. For if he doth not find his way back by the light of your prayer, he might be lost forever."

"How do you pray for someone who has become a stranger to you?"

"Love Him as you would love yourself. It is sad that not many take the time to recognize how to see eye-to-eye in relationships as mountains block sight of each other unless on level ground. Finding this kind of love before one *builds* is a necessity.

What you need know, Liam, is the further you enter love's doorway from the *Book of Life*, the more truth will grow to allow you to retain its substance from within and *build*. It is here a full life for love causes all to stand to cast away fears, and this is what keeps the door open for our prayers.

Read steadily from it each day and you will grow into the existence of what is real; a life fit together that reaches out to all where loving one another shall point to *level* holy ground.

For within the breath of The Holy Spirit, we become accustomed to a foundational attitude. He grows to last forever as we're allowed our new beginnings."

I marvel at the Monsignor's words, "That's why I've come. I've been building without fully understanding my foundation. Everything I've learned has not been set in order. Why, I've had no place to turn that would answer me back in full relationship!"

"Hmmm, what you say must be within the Great One's timing. For, this is why we've been making copies of the *Book of Life* for the past few years. This copy, Prince Liam, by our Lord's grace, be for you.

Soon it shall be time to learn from its word, and then the news will spread to all subjects throughout the province of Calington. They too will know of its order, and then the truth behind our gatherings will bear a light for all generations to come. It will be known by the essence of its perfection as a true guide."

For some reason the witches map catches my eye and I snatch it up in hand, "We won't be needing this anymore." I'm about to tear it, but suddenly an overwhelming peace comes upon me. I then notice the Monsignor and Jerome have joined in prayer. "What is it?"

Jerome looks over and calmly explains, "You can never destroy that which is evil with man's wisdom. For it only makes it stronger."

The Monsignor then opens the *Book of Life* he was presenting to me and places it on his desk. It rests near a large pitcher of water upon a small round tray surrounded by ceramic cups.

"Majesty, this book is to be read consistently for us to continue to grow together as a body within its order. If you were to tear up this map with a show of force, spirits would be released to cause more harm. Yet, based on what I know about the Great One from reading His *Book of Life,* I can place it within the book's structure and watch Him answer."

The Monsignor then places the map within the pages of the *Book of Life*. I watch as the map suddenly bursts into flames, but before I can get to the pitcher of water, it quickly turns to ashes before us all. Yet, my copy of the book remains unburned. I am astonished!

Jerome then informs: "It is by the pattern of the person behind this book, through purity of light, that all evil gets destroyed."

"Then entering into its life as read, this is how we become a part of it."

"Transformation from being married to death, broken by the pattern of life has begun. For now we're alive, building line-upon-line by the completed foundation of the Great One. For threads have been stitched into a full garment, completely given to breaths knowing life within its essence, as now there is light by His sight.

As when that which is deadly old becomes known before the Great One loses hold, His help gives vision upon request 'til all darkness be wrestled away.

Evil only loses its place in the purity of virtue found upon its living pages, as when kept alive with understanding we live it out. Then those who believe in the reality of the Great One's book will know eternal life."

The Monsignor closes the book and extends it towards me. Reaching forward I grasp it in-hand and immediately take it into my bosom with embrace. "I thank you!"

Jerome then comments: "The *Book of Life* will plot a course to know how to find your true love when any trouble comes. He is alive and will open the way to go by giving you a single mind."

"I will read it and know of its life."

The Monsignor rises, "Prince Liam, my office is yours."

"Wait! Where are you going? I still have questions!"

The Monsignor gives me a reassuring look, "You hold all you need within your grasp."

I stare in disbelief as he and Jerome exit, closing the door behind them. Now I realize that I have a choice, other than the ones that are familiar to me.

I look down at what I am holding in my hands, knowing the *Book of Life* will not only be light for me, but to all those who are able to receive it.

As I slowly open the book, I immediately get the feeling of *difference*.

"From now on, things will never be the same. There shall be place for stability in an unstable world."

VIII

"After reading for only a short while, I am enthralled with its content. It's not long before verses start to jump out, and as they do, doors from my past begin to gradually open. I soon realize that it is His gentle touch within my soul.

The Spirit of the Great One reveals all by visiting me in a warm, loving manner. His gradual building fire enters setting me aglow within. There is a lining up of events by the truth of Him, which brings comfort to heal my hurts. It is as though a portal into the pages of this book has opened within me.

I surrender to the timing of His purpose. It causes me to acknowledge Him in place of my old thoughts. The truth I thought as *sound*, apart from the heart of His presence, was found to choke me within walls of isolation. I see. Without the light of His better way of understanding, I have been kept miserable.

For I was slow to recognize that I was around abuse when all seemed safe. Though when weighing out this balance, more is reveled. *Why, it is out of the mouth through spoken words we enter streams of !ife or death.*' Yet, which is which I've not yet learned so here I must be cautious. For only in life doth healing take place, and from this path, I do not wish to stray.

His Spirit has been patient with me. All is being revealed in the pages of His word, the wisdom of His continual gentleness keeps me calm.

By their example, the priests have helped me to see balance in relationships while among them. For I have entered into the riches of even more depth of warmth. He is the lover of my soul who resolves my conflict out of the midst of where darkness once took its toll—and while in this light I am never alone.

Everything's being restored as my thoughts are brought to order from the Spirit of His mind.

All from the marvelously glorious words of truth I read. For where there is order, there is more room to contain life. Gradually, I feel it well up as the joy of a solid foundation rings with truth inside my soul.

Reflection of droplets and eternal truth add to my picture. I'm gaining a whole new stage of life which I know entreats me deeper. It causes me to come alive with a vision I've not yet known to grasp before. My roots start to stretch within wisdom's rich and fertile soil taking hold. Then I come to this new life understanding. I am growing to a place of safety, one I knew not before. It helps me to make better choice where I come alive in breaths of life.

My thoughts are loaded with the voices of Holy Angels, as though praying right through me. They reveal...*'How it is the Great One's strength that will lift me out of any pit I may fall into. For He dines with me and I with Him, as I open to His knock upon my heartfelt cords.'*

Next I see how using the force of my own strength only exhausts. Could there be a way I know not of, where I don't have to give it my all?

Here, moved further away from the opening I have first entered, I'm found to dig even deeper. It was through my own poor choice I got into this mess, which brought the taste of death. Oh! The turmoil that is within my soul. How is this going to change me into anything new?

I now have sight. In order to break any pattern I must learn to observe my actions. I make a mental log of how I have related with those around and search out why?

Answers come: I connect with everyone at the root of my relationships. At their very depths, angels bring me on a fierce journey of thought, revealing what I'm able to bear.

I must draw nearer to the Great One as a matter of need. He unfolds His path before me. Now in the midst of my uncertainties there are new choices I can make. *'It is a must that I continue to press on!'* Yet, the Great One, who is greater than I, shall He not change me? I rely upon His Spirit to place new flesh upon my bones.

All is gentle within His touch as long as I remain and trust. Guided down this path I truly learn to trust while reaching out for Him to grasp my hand. Was there a bond in love when I spoke the truth that allowed for grace to find the Great One's light? Would His abilities be known to me above my own? For even in other relations without order revealed I've had it all and I'm fed up with it. I need more than what I've known!

I now hear my Lord's voice from His words I read, they come alive and bring me peace about what's going on in Calington. At last I am in the midst of serenity. Love and truth have been brought together in the power of His sacrifice with sight for direction, but this time there is balance of sanity in my step.

Heartfelt praise bursts forth from my heart as in an expression of song. *'I am purposed to break the surface of the soil and enter in beyond the door–wait, now I'm experiencing His light. It has come into focus by being slowed to stillness at last.'* The door to my heart opens that much more.

I adore and reflect on coming to know Him more, thus as my trust turns to peace, forward I grow. All becomes magnified–and pondering over what is happening brings a harvest of joyous exaltation. My hand has found His grip again; my heart His presence.

I exceedingly rejoice in the acceptance of the Great One's embrace and intoxicating laughter sends deeper touch, all by His Spirit within my soul.

'It's not about how much I love Him, but about how much I am willing to let Him love me that counts.'

Slowed down to a pause more stillness of moment comes, I encounter embrace. For I am known when in the midst of being one with His love.

How could I have glossed over all of this truth in my lessons as youth? I see now. It is the practical application of His words of truth added to personal experience which allows relations to rest upon our Lord's loving Spirit. I just needed to be patient long enough to see Him bring everything together in order to comprehend the beauty of His light.

The Great One has given me a sound mind and the liar has been pushed out. It is the high substance of truth I'm to focus on, who He is within full character. Otherwise I just reach out and thin air awaits in whisps as I miss with whom I am relating.

In the dark pit, I fell back to the lie with no Great One to call upon and all was lost. I see now. When love and truth do not come together, suffering happens.

Why, there's a process in the formation of light! The Great One's order brings me further understanding which directs by truth to end all darkened plights. My sight has light beyond my flesh. Power was once stolen, taken away by the lie of being in control that deceived me from my life!

My vision speaks. I invited a pretense of truth outside the Great One's pattern wherein lay destruction I've faced. For willpower can never cleanse, it only masks over true spiritual battles that lay unseen beneath man's wisdom.

The truth is more than a one time experience! It is something we need to eat to sustain us.

I marvel as I recognize what happened with my father, for false messages presented as truth brings about evil to confuse and remove us from life. At this revelation, I feel a groaning within that I let out, releasing what gives way from expressions of seeing light break darkness inside my soul.

'Stacks of gold, very cold, from under a sea of sacrificial blood. Walking on a tight rope that's waiting to be cut. Cut right through the edge of time, it once was yours, it once was mine. There were wishes in this age-old scheming well, in truth, plainly there for all with sight to see—desiring to possess that which was real—Silent screams, they fill the night

too frightening to hear. For if we did we'd hear ourselves and disrupt our endless rest of death.'

I'm now in a sweat. These words have come out from me, but not yet in touch with them I bow my head and with their meaning only half taken in–I look away.

It is because of their starkness I read on, desiring to escape my emotions for fear of something I might not be ready to see.

Miraculously, within the next few lines of verse, all of my fears are calmed and my thoughts and emotions are brought together to process my feelings at last.

'I see now, when left to myself, with all that is going on in the kingdom. A painful place tis me to be.'

Finally, healing has come as I know the Great One has been tearfully watching. He is even here for me now, kept away by false deceiving spirits upon the wind no more!

'Am I still of my father or do now I serve the Great One?' This question has come to mind.

I'm now found in awe of this storehouse of wisdom 'til another truth takes me by surprise,

'Beware of the dark spirit that'll bid for your affections against what be dear and true? Even to serve the Lord while resting falsely without true peace and call this grace, is its ploy.'

Hmmm! Will a conception question filled with knowledge bring me any closer to the Spirit of the Great One in this book, or set up a stumbling block to keep me from His love?

Keeping eyes on the Great One to draw life is the way in spite of what surrounds. His Spirit must be my strength in place of what I have considered my own.

It is all the prayers I've heard, *'Prayers of the priests that opened the door for me to cry out to You—They never gave up on me and neither do You. I have found in You the help I seek when troubles arise. I'm not to run but face them!*

Knowing You are the One my Lord who'll bring trust of Your protection. By the fact, You are the Greatest of all. You turn darkness out, fully bringing me to light in the midst of all storms. For it is Your most excellent Spirit that rules overall.

Where have You been all my life and what has kept me from You?'

The Great One now rests upon the throne of my heart. He, as head, is the picture of my joy complete. As completely seeing within the light of His Holiness, I watch other spirits fall way. Lies are now exposed and darkness peeled back as I'm *stilled* to notice one more leaving me in awe.

This dark spirit is revealed to have a place that has kept my brother and father at bay from me. The spirit seems small, like the dragon before I crushed its head in the valley. Yet, still it takes me by surprise, *'A jealous spirit. Me? Where?'*

It is the love my brother Ed and my father have for one another. I've been carrying this lying spirit and doing great damage, it even now bends my heart to humility.

'Oh, how it has harmed my relationship with them!

Foul and dark secret hidden away from me, hidden no more! Though thou felt so comfortable, as even a part of my bond, lifted away from me you'll be 'til you drain me no more. Now I lay you down defeated, burned away by the advances of my Great One's loving truth as He holds my heart in hand.'

I'm found to rest within His light of joy once more. My fondest affections are of grace upon grace, found at last back in my own prepared purpose of place.

The dragon is as big as we make him, within power of strength from our own choice of mind and capable of rapid growth.

'I've been jealous of their relationship for all these years and never shared in the joy of their love for one another. Forgive my selfishness!

I see that when darkness is carried, it blocks knowing the depth of truth within pure light. Oh how I grieve, but not to despair—yet rather to first rays of light, like anticipation of sunrise at dawn.

This causes me to shine forth with gladness.

'Great One, patient with me You've been. Loving me all this while throughout my shortsightedness, You have suffered long. It is by understanding this that I draw nearer to receive even more of Your patient love.

I see the payment of Your sacrifice, its meaning clearly shines through even more. You in me and me in You, 'til at last there is the power of Your harmony between us.'

I watch another shadow fall away and become aware that growth has taken place inside the members of my *being* as tears of gladness find themselves to leave my eyes. I am found so gratefully lifted in joy beyond words to describe.

Then, while still enjoying the presence of the Great One, a sudden impulse comes over me. *'I'm to seek to mend my family relationships!'*

However, having grown within the Great One's love, straight way I recognize a spirit that hovers around trying to land in my mind. It wants to enter to keep out other thoughts of the Great One's workings, the ones I've just learned to discern and embrace as He has just planted a little more of His Spirit in me which I can rely. He has removed my old restless nature, no longer doth it stand in my way. The dark cloud has been lifted and at last I've regained my sight. Be gone dragon!

I know in whom I trust by grace and choose to wait for all the more. It is a must! I shall wait on the timing of the Great One's change, upon this matter as well, or out of step with Light of Peace once more I'll be.

His Word has now been most solidly lain. For seeing deeper, my vision reveals myself as once a wilted flower in the garden of life.

'Wasn't I on a dead branch when He was passing by? Stopping to know me with all of His love 'til lifting me to be a part of His thriving vine?'

Now that His Great Spirit gives spacious place, I grow and graciously He pushes out another spirit to no longer float within my mind. My soul is now sustained in true substance of purity. Again, I have found honesty to join me to the truth, the Great One's love fills me. Confused hollows now become saturated with His free gift of whole life, known only by His word. One day a darkened mind will be no more, and here is where I shall remain in bloom with hopeful smile from ear to ear.

'The Great One has always been there to answer my questions for a sound mind, I just had to see my need to search him out and understand His answer to my calls.

Hidden away they laid 'til my bond could be more fully understood by the truth of Himself.'

No peace. I must not move. I'm to wait for His timing which is peace, as He is peace. I'll not survive in the manner of a childish spirit and remain the same forever. I'll grow to know Him in each of my moments 'til I'm all the way through, as a step-by-step progression of change which will lead to a deep rooted maturity within His vine.

'When I make a poor choice, I am like a loose thread in a garment become caught. If I keep traveling in the wrong direction I'll become undone. I see now that the reality I call upon to back me up is what really shapes me.'

Do I fight to stay conscious of the Great One's pattern for living, or grow into a bad flow where my inner life would slowly get stolen away by currents of death again?

"Why, I'd be left depleted. I must not give into my old devices." Here, I am humbled to ask my Lord for help to deliver me from the mire of a pit in which I sink.

Finally, seen in place of my old affections, I'm to flee to the embrace of the Great One's Spirit where I've learned to put my trust in the power of divine faithfulness to newly be changed. Now throughout any conflict that might befall, I shall remain with my heart in His love and grow rather than be swallowed by further darkness.

'I will not call upon spirits of thought any longer that kept my past uneasy, I must face them with Your Spirit, or I too will handle future situations on my own.'

Led to purposeful clarity of mind, I'm directed not to take action using my own wisdom. I'm to continue to wait for the Great One's timing to take effect. For I know it is He who will restore my family, as He did me to sanity.

Within my powerlessness, the weight of an abusive burden is lifted and here I rest. Now, there is a new found freedom in the air. The Spirit of the Great One fills the chambers of my soul. His brilliance has pierced the dark veil with protection of new life.

'At last, I have been liberated!'"

I hear knocking which disrupts my thoughts, then realize it is at the door. All at once I'm again in the study of the Monsignor. The knocking continues so I call out, "Whose there?"

"Liam, it's Jerome. Are you all right?"

"Come see."

Jerome enters, but when he draws near, he stops and starts to smile at me. "What is it?" I ask.

"You are smiling from the inside-out."

"I thought we just talked with the Great One, I never knew you could actually know Him."

"You've been reading Him three days without food or drink, yet you are still refreshed as foretold by prophecy. Your transformation has begun.

Come now, you must reveal yourself within the love of the priesthood first, then within the Great One's timing to the whole world!"

I think it a bit odd the way Jerome is carrying on, but then watch as he walks over and opens the doors to the study.

The Monsignor leads the way as a sea of priests quietly file into the room just to look upon me and receive possible instruction.

They share in my joy, which I know to be flowing from within me. Then unanimously they say agreeing, "The deliverer!"

I am surprised at this and protest, "Only the anointed One can be the deliverer! Now enough talk of prophecy."

"But the fire is in you..."

"As He is in me, by the same Spirit, He is available to all that agree to let Him burn."

"Majesty, but you being the first born prince in line to be king fulfills prophecy," were the Monsignor's words.

Next the proverb comes to me, *"It is the glory of God to conceal a matter: but the honor of kings to search it out.*

I'm so in love with the Great One, yet there were parts of the Book of Life I have not finished." I decide I must read on 'til knowing the whole story before addressing the brethren again. "If I am the deliverer, then the Great One will bring it to pass.

For I have seen love and truth come together in a balanced way within my heart giving balance to see life's light come by the verses I have read.

Let us be reminded that in studying the truth of the Great One's way 'minus His love' it invites rather than pushes out darkness.

Remember that when we are dimmed by distractions which seek to engulf, dragons will always be there to retaliate. For their teeth have purpose and they don't want to lose ground while they bite as hungry bellies await from the confusion they have brought.

Our requests, as I understand it, must be made to the Great One. As it is within His wisdom—to wait on how all will unfold.

After all isn't it He who answers within His own timing, work in all to anticipate each divine appointment...

Wherein, with better understanding, we learn to know Him who brings everything to pass?

Inside His gratitude, are we not grateful? I for one have been delivered from such a beast. The Lord's glorious power, which I marvelously beheld, shall bring love adding to the affection of many eyes.

Now, let us have a divine wait which will be best on behalf of all. For it will allow us to meet within our Great One's appointed timing—and bring peace as renewal against any darkness in the air. Know, we do not have to defend the truth by forcing it, but rather we are to just share it as we live within its pattern, while we grow to deeper comprehend the story."

The priests look on in awe, as my words have been strung together as costly pearls. Yet, I remain unaware of their great value—or how they are affecting them.

"You all know that it is the Great One who works the truth within us. We are incapable of bringing about lasting change. For what is corrupted cannot make itself incorruptible!

'Hear me.' Keeping consciously aware of the Great One is our example of this. For it is within His light that we're found to have sight in the making of purest choice.

Is this not where our darkness is kept out? Is this not where we learn to trust to ask Him to meet our every thirst, for change to take place from within us?

For, He is the One who has paved the path to His kingdom. This is why the pressures of this world are unable to invade the truth, when we call out, as our Great One knows what is best. For from within the life of His own perfect blood. He brings gifts bringing change to us. Doth not His strength keep us from withdrawing or freezing up?

We may feel a discomfort and groan in our souls, as we let go of what we thought was our own personal desires. Where love did not flow, but confusion finally gives way when loving His boundaries of peace, which has far greater power.

Have we not learned by the better vision of His life now within us? How His light produced entrance beneath all lies, leaving a truly new life, with a sweeter taste where all press on."

I pause and reflect before the brethren who are all in anticipation of what is to come with hungry eyes.

"Even more complete, and deeper than this, I know the pattern of unfailing love and living truth always comes together. Giving off a real and balanced light for the widest perception of a most full life. Denial no longer has hold here. As fullness allows my mind to grow to comprehend the Great One."

My dark thoughts are kept at bay. Thus, receiving a burst of strength, I now know of being released to grow to the fullest of any relationship. As letting go of pain, wherein I had only strife, brilliance of the Great One's Company now comforts.

"I am made aware my breaths are prayers, joining all to their life's source, flowing from the Great One Himself.

I see now. I am to be still that He may continue to craft, but how?'

The eyes of the priests continue to be upon me as my eyes look beyond full of light.

"Lord, You are alive and I know You're inside. It's Your love which fills my soul. I am on fire!

There is completion in knowing You care to carry out Your work in me. The fact You've only just begun thrills me to my bones because I rest in the trust of Your timing above my own. Still more for me to see—Your grace is fulfilled in my weakness! Draw me closer to You in the midst of my flaws—as I am at a loss to fully comprehend them.

It is far too great for me to understand, as my sight is less than Thine. I am glad for this life which You have given, as I no longer can deny our heart's beating as one. In awe, I am at the wonder of this truth. I want to know no other worth. No choice other than to comply."

I burn with passion from inside 'til out comes what I've taken in by love through depths of newly searching eyes. All at once I cry out, "The Great One has just revealed His name to me!"

Turning to the Monsignor, I look for guidance before slumping forward and placing my hand upon his desk.

He responds in a gentle manner, "You are only to use the Great One's name when He leads you to do so in His power.

For Liam, I want you to know this ahead of time: His name will continue to mean salvation as all darkness will be brought to the hope of light for everyone.

Now know it! This is the given sign of your purpose fulfilled. As you, Prince Liam, are the deliverer."

"I don't even know Him well enough to use His name. How will I know when it is time?"

"His name will come out of your mouth by His own Spirit, then you'll know it is time, but be reassured He will be holding you completely together from within His confidence. Otherwise, you'll return to speaking with pride which has nothing to do with the Great One's Spirit."

I grow suddenly weary and find myself collapsing in my mentor's chair. The Monsignor then encourages me to drink some water handed me from one of the ceramic cups. Afterwards, he invites me to be placed in his quarters, but I assure him that the dorm will do fine. All at once I give way, as my head folds with my chin touching my chest.

The priests gather around as I'm met with a sea of hands that carry my joyful body through the corridors that become a blur.

I hear parts of sentences that I can't quite make out. Their voices seem muffled as I float while groaning with gladness 'til finally they lower me in my bunk.

It is now nighttime and again I start to hear the priests pray as they kneel at their bedsides.

The first priest speaks with a low tone of voice: "Oh Lord, grant that Queen Mary shall walk again. Bring Your touch by the power of Your great love. Heal her spine and comfort her in her time of need."

The next voice is filled with excitement: "Oh Lord, thank You for the power of Your strength that sustains me throughout the day. Thank You for Your love and the love of my brothers. Cause me to be patient as You reveal to us how Prince Liam is to fulfill his role as deliverer. Let it be made known to us quickly!"

My mind becomes settled as reality becomes a deeper comfort than all the racing thoughts of excitement that has just happened over the past few days. The prayer continues– "Oh Lord, my heart is breaking over the many thoughts I have that are not from You. I haven't the strength to carry on within the pull of this dark tide which even now pulls at my soul to ever wear on me. Be my strength during this time of transition, I know it is you who must change me to truly be changed. Change me, my love. For I know I'll never be ready unless you craft me. Change me, my love, and I will be changed forever."

After hearing the words of their faith, the revelation comes to me: *the*

Book of Life is more than real, IT IS ALIVE!

"Your words are alive, oh Great One. Hold our future and continue to meet with us as I know thou be living.

Carry me, I ask, through what I am to face on all of the morrows!"

I then dose off with peace as His truth takes firm hold. My thoughts burst upward towards heaven, washing me within His embrace. Kept I am, by a love newly discovered by the purity of His blood. For now He is the power, glory, and lifter of my head.

IX

$\mathcal{T}$he sun looms with the haze of another humid morn. In the queen's chamber at Calington Castle, a meeting takes place. Two trusted members from the proconsul whisper their views concerning the affairs of the most recent turn of events.

Sir Kneed speaks up before the queen and the duke of Slatsberg: "I believe King Henry's rule has grown to where he now hears only himself instead of the voice of truth whom he serves. His example has become most unruly. Even now it threatens the balance of our kingdom."

Mother next voices her opinion, "I see the wind of a certain fear has been creeping in over the courage of the Great One's voice nowadays. This is a crucial time in our now vulnerable kingdom. We must proceed with caution as to not bring division to it."

Back at the monastery, sorting through some thoughts, I find myself before the Great One concerning what is to happen next. For after such powerful embrace from the Great One, understanding with clarity comes prevalent to mind.

From new heights on His Mountain, I can truly see much further out over the valley. Something starts to stir within me concerning father; it's time to pray.

Meanwhile–Sir Kneed and the duke of Slatsberg look to one another then back to mother at bedside. After things settle down, she continues, "The reason I've called you here…"

An abrupt knock is heard at the door, opening to reveal the king who has something behind his back; a dozen roses. He stops and stares as he realizes the queen has company. After overcoming his initial surprise, the king barks out "What is this… a secret meeting?!"

"A mere visitation between friends, my dear. That is all."

"Oh, I see. Excuse me, I'll go."

"Wait a minute. Now that you are here, why have you come?"

The king extends his hand from behind his back with the bouquet. "These are for you. I've missed you, Mary. I thought it would be nice to have a few moments together."

"Roses are my favorite."

"I remember it well."

"Oh Henry, all would be worthwhile if we can just start over again.

The queen looks over to the members of the proconsul with a suggestive look in her eyes, they then give invitation to the king, "Won't you join us, your majesty?"

It is lunchtime at the monastery. About noon. Three more days seem to have just flown by. It has been a real luxury to have had some time to read and meditate upon the *Book of Life*. In reflection on what's been read, I'd say it was time well spent. For now I've come to know our Great One in a deeper way.

I must admit, the result of this *while* has answered many unanswered questions.

Now seated in the dining hall, among the many brethren a more vivid picture comes to mind. For their fellowship of presence holds a strong bond.

In this light of love there is camaraderie as all listen to each other. Gaining insight into their conversation, I see how people do not enjoy a life that lacks in having sight of full reality.

This adds to my understanding wherein built upon the simplicity of their company and brought to deep meditation from many pages read, the book further increases my sight.

I see now that suffering exists because there is evil in the world which prevents full sight of living word. It festers in the off-balance of falsehood, advancing within dark pockets towards us when the mind is dim.

Masking over the universe, it has the advantage to feed upon all while unaware. This predator cannot stand on its own strength, but hides everywhere outside the presence of our Great One's light. Feeding off dissatisfied miseries by leaving turmoil within others, it seeks to find its strength.

Whenever an internal structure of balance becomes threatened before the Great One, what is in the order of good becomes deflected with clouds as we are tried. Traps are set, just as a maze of what is dark blots out light.

Dragons thrive within this darkness. Forceful they are when challenging our efforts trying to disturb visions of soundness.

I would even say they thrive when throwing what is good out of order, and if given enough time, they'd draw one completely away from pure light that sight be made obscure.

I get a glimpse at an example of this: A part of the nature of evil is to call what is good *evil*. Through its relentless taunting 'til hindered from receiving choices that are good, picked off we can become when isolated.

Recalling the actions of my father before drink, I reflect upon how he has been unruly in character lately as compared to how his life was in the past. He is under evil attack. I next conclude that evil must only work from within distorted patterns.

His nature is filled with hate. It is due to frustrations of anger as he cannot see beyond the spell of the golden goblet. This must be where his choices are made towards the lie of other spirits that feast, and this darkness doth not allow him to find the way. Rather, he embraces the dragon which hides in the dark. For he cannot see, he steps in and out of its mouth.

Acting upon spirits that lurk without light, pain feeds a fuel that drives him. Choices be made which propose life, but powers behind his actions cause a rage which baits him unto a death he cannot face.

My poor father is not able to accept any blame as his actions take him into knowing uneasy choices that be dark. Adversely, they grow to cut him off from outside the balance of any self control. For he remembers not it be myth, but a gift that holds him in place.

"Great One, send Your light to him. Break the spirits that keep him frozen and away from Your loving warmth."

I look to the brethren I dine with and really see their countenances as good. It suddenly comes to me, the Great One is in control of everything. It is having found His path I am with Him in the midst of my suffering.

I will fully come to know the existence of His pattern of life at last; one where I'm acknowledged in what was a growingly distasteful world.

Now within gratitude of what has been done for me, the waters from the dark tide are held back in my life. All that lingers within the shadows is kept at bay. I have an unshakeable place to meet with the Lord and put forth my trust. Having come out from sharing the same old bread of men. I now know that I have a feast ahead of me in a reality of depth that will not fail.

The Great One's pattern establishes a place for stability, which stands to give reason. For having an outside view allows us to see and experience torments of suffering within life's staleness. Our quest is to end anything, which prevents an acknowledgment to end this evil.

The Great One within His heart of compassion, leaves Himself open to take the place of our torments from suffering. For He dwells with us, always through the truth of His embrace. He lives and moves and breathes, and we enjoy the benefits of His sacrifice. Him being alive inside us, this is proof enough to know He cares to keep us loyal to His established word, and this brings comfort to all in His kingdom.

In the midst of our anguish He is the place to turn. We can actually embrace our pain without any fear; as His nurturing grows to love life in place of death.

Through the discovery of this action of mercy, I bring my pain to Him, and he teaches me to know Him better. For, within the safety of His pattern, there is an expulsion of all torment from my pride which causes a surrender, as it is ever before me 'til suffering this trial no more.

Why, on every occasion, all that pained me on my search caused changes to occur. Finding the Great One's love to answer, and take the place of all discomforts, when responding to my call. He grants access to a kingdom of life; as all advance 'til there be no more darkness to disrupt any from rest.

I see being taught Him, within each new call, allows me to better know the truth of who He is. For in discovering His character, within all patience, I understand Him at His depths. He grants real maturity, which grows in sincere peace, especially when set in an authority that leaves me not anxious. I then realize, it has been by invitation we have called to Him to come and live with us.

I compare being outside the Great One's pattern to being lost in the woods. I suffer here from the torment of not knowing the way. 'Til I am comforted by seeing the true path that belongs to Him once again. For here I find joy from the peace of mind He brings–that of knowing where I am going. Thus my torment is expelled while passing on from the trees to the safety of His path. I am no longer lost throughout my suffering, but am comforted by His love.

I like being among honest men, seasoned with grace, who know how to speak the truth in love. It is like seeing the true path to continue my journey, and this comforts me. Now, challenged again, I must grow to where my confidence lay more in the Great One's abilities; even above my own. I shall find my place within His timing, by allowing Him to fulfill my purpose within His gift to bring me life, then preparation shall be complete.

I shall wait to know His pace; then all things will come into view according to prophecy. No matter how things look in my own eyes. My thoughts must bring me back to where I return to the path of remembering the way to go; for, while walking in His light, always there is the warmth of His way.

Eyes are upon me it seems, as though my true inside character of the Great One is being tested. I then remember how He has become my trust in the little things, which enhance the image of who I am, and here I am held together.

Though the question still arises like sun breaking forth at dawn from night, *"Have I honestly touched with relating to the Great One in everything?"* I mean the way the brethren appear to do so without effort.

Well, according to the *Book of Life*, His reflection of grace covers me. Yet, there must still be places I lack in other unknown areas of my life? Such as using will-power, which only distracts from hearing God's gentle voice.

I next hear my heart within my mind, *"Draw me closer and keep me on Your path, for now I know Your authority rules over any efforts of my own.*

'Make me more like You Oh Great One.' For You have risen in glory from the dead. Your proof of seal of promise of love is displayed in Your great power of sacrifice. You have lain the true root by this seed that all can rise within this light of truth."

Everyone enters by this door that joins, making us family, for the sanity of love cannot be ignored. Thus we are brought into unity within the fulfillment of grace as You are at the center restoring all to life; humble enough to call with a desire for peace.

"From now on, before encountering others, I'll have to consider Your way. For touching Your pattern before proceeding is wise. No longer will people back away from a lack of consideration, as being changed I myself have answered this love and call. For now Your Spirit is my guide."

With my mind refreshed I smell the aroma of some food being passed around. Now at peace, I take a helping of scrambled eggs, sausage, and wheat cakes, as they come by. Keeping the flow moving, I next pass the baskets to the others around the large round table.

What a blessing it is to serve as well as be served. Although, I must admit, making my bed this morn was found to be a bit humbling; it did take me quite a few tries. It hasn't been about focusing in on any one meaning that has brought all together for me. It was spending time with the priests that made me aware of the fact I was in the presence of the Great One.

My spirit suddenly tries to figure everything out. Yet, now I remember, it is necessary to wait on the Great One. I must remain still, and within His moment. He is the One, who will reveal all mysteries, as the gift of His presence I do enjoy. If I remember my patience be within His timing.

As, when at rest, He meets each with deep embrace.

Claude, a large burley man, folds his oversized hands and begins a conversation of grace.

"Thank You our Great One for all we've received, watch over us this day, and guide us to a vision of You more than we even more."

While I am eating, I hear bits of conversation. Soon after, I tune into the fact, the brethren are fanning one another's fire inside a reality of faith; their flame is strong.

Moved deeper, by attitude, the Great One's presence joins our company. My newly acquired appetite becomes whet; so I join in their open conversation, which happens to be of a religious nature.

By clearing my throat all heads are invited to turn towards me. Then what's upon my heart is made known to all.

"When sharing compulsively have we not seen how religion always strips one of their character? Leaving them without their own identity?"

There is a pause, then James one of the brothers at the table adds, "...and dependent on the leadership of the church rather than upon the Great One, which the church is following. It may appear this way, but all the facts must be presented."

Some of the other brethren join in. My original remark has started a sort of rippling effect.

Peter, a priest who has been considered to be the greatest servant of all, living closest to the Great One states:

"I know what you're saying, but listen to James. First, what must be seen is there's a difference in this place. For when each one is a priest we all share in full reality; wherein to know Our Great One is to know His church.

For we identify in sharing the promise of the Great One's love, with encouragement, before one another; as witness."

Claude, "Aren't we to trust the leadership of the church to point us to this witness, for as little children do we not enter the kingdom of heaven?"

Peter, "Yet, once inside the kingdom there's growth in the knowledge of grace towards being complete."

Luke, "All that is evil would not have us see this, as power of unity with forgiveness is a real danger to it."

I notice that everyone is polite, they speak in turn, which makes me feel secure by the structure of their lives. It is next pointed out to me by Peter, "In leadership there's a guarantee of an uninterrupted succession of faith. This is where the truth, from its beginning, be kept like an unmovable seed that continues to grow.

A vote within the priesthood, which mercifully cannot be altered from perfection, guaranties this. For if change were to happen within any variables from its original intent; the truth would dissipate, as in the nature of a lie held to light."

I next ask, "Could creation itself become undone and fall from the sky if everyone was to believe a lie?"

In response Matthew joins us, "Being one, and centered around our Great One. This is the kind of relationship that encourages, as pressures of life are kept back, when character is built in an atmosphere that holds all in place. Yield to the pace of His pattern, by soundness of mind, and let His balance establish embrace. Then shall come deeper love for everyone as mercy is what establishes.

Life becomes enhanced by this kind of growth, which moves towards great understanding, it leaves quality living for us; as better choices are made when we are nurtured.

We relate to Him, within a deeper vision of who He is, when knowing His love discovers our hearts. For in discovering deep mercy to triumph over judgment, should we drift, we know we have a place to return to Him, and this kind of love makes it hard to stray."

John interjects, "Substance is the key. We need the Great One's reality without holes in it. For in relating with Him, as a part of His family, we have better sight when relating with others."

My heart stirs, "The *Book of Life!* His word, through the Great One's Spirit, places all together by your witnesses around me; even as He fills in a lot of answers now.

Studying too, helps me to know the love of truth. And, even better, I talk with Him who is alive within it. Just as He is alive in you, and this sharpens. I too must walk hand in hand with Him, as this is the proof of His image reflected upon my heart, which directs."

Mark interrupts, "I can see a lot of weeds have been pulled up at breakfast today. As for sure, this is a message that we will want to bring to other countries, but I do believe it's time to pull some up in the garden as well." We all break out in agreeable laughter and clean up.

After our dining area is set in order, with much love and respect for one another, we start for the garden. I know that my father wants me in prison and my mother may never walk again, but in the midst of all my troubles I'm bubbling with joy. I could get used to this place, even if I had to stay 'til my father...

"Prince Liam, Prince Liam!" The Monsignor catches my attention upon reaching the door. He approaches and I recognize the messenger who is with Him.

"Sire, the queen informs it is safe for you to come back to the castle. She requests audience with you at once."

"Then I will go to her."

I am disappointed that I must leave so soon.

The brethren look on in disbelief 'til Claude breaks the silence, "So soon my brother?"

Then James adds, "The Great One's timing is sometimes abrupt, at others gradual, but we must learn to know them all."

John shares his heart, "Your love for her is very strong, yet I feel it is your obligation to a higher honor that too has your heart."

Matthew with tears in his eyes, "I'm gonna miss ya Liam." We all exchange hugs and then I am ready.

Accompanied to the front gate, two horses are ready and waiting for us, but then I notice there is no accompaniment of guards; which thought I dismiss, as we are supposedly at a time of peace and not war.

Now with my attention towards the brethren, I assure my fellow priests that I will come and visit. They respond by telling me that they will keep me in their prayers.

We mount up with the wind at our backs. I take this as surety the Great One is with us. Then next join the messenger on his ride. He remains relatively quiet.

I am in anticipation that justice has been carried out; the Great One has heard our prayers.

Later on, when the wind dies down a bit, it is quickly noted how the sun grows hot upon my back. By the Great One's lead we come to a watering hole and dismount.

As I turn leading my horse, suddenly I am taken by surprise coming face to face with a large poisonous serpent.

The Great One's Spirit causes me not to be afraid while speaking through my thoughts to this venomous snake. *"Leave this vessel alone!"*

Immediately, it turns and slithers away. I'm next brought to the realization of how this serpent had me cold. How grateful I become and am quick to thank the Great One with a full royal worth, I know I now have. He has been merciful in this situation, and sensing my life spared, a new found confidence rests within me. I next turn round to see an arrow pointed right at me. "If you're going to shoot I'm ready."

"Do you really mistrust your father that much?"

"When it comes to him I don't know what to believe anymore, but I do know that the Great One has a plan for me."

"This arrow was for the serpent majesty," he then relaxes his bow. Throughout the remainder of the journey there is a sweet tasting Spirit in the air. I sense much has been accomplished in my absence.

However; upon arrival at the castle I'm steered clear from being spotted at the main gate. The queen's messenger quickly instructs me to use the secret passageway after crossing the draw bridge.

My countenance drops, as a sickening feeling tells me I was kept from a complete picture of the truth. Remembering that the Great One is in control, rather than protest, I choose to continue to enjoy Him by following the path at hand.

The messenger starkly looks over; then finishes his orders by accompanying me to the entrance and handing me a torch. Afterward he informs, "Go straight to your mother."

With the torch now lit, I enter straight way through the secret passage and quickly find my way to her chambers from behind the walls.

My mother is alone when I spy through the peephole. I knock at the passage door, as not to startle her.

"You may enter."

The wall creeks open, and after hanging my torch, I joyfully slip in from behind the bookcase. My mother and queen is lying in bed, excitedly I go to her. Gladly, with open arms, she greets me with a hug. But, sensing her to be strangely rigid, I pull away.

"What is it mother, what's wrong?"

"I will be straight with you Liam. Your strange disappearance, around the time of my accident, has not gone unnoticed."

I keep my composure, hoping I am not going to hear what will come next. Waiting upon the Great One, I politely take a breath and speak from my concerns, "Say on."

"It would be better if my accident were your fault, I'll pardon you, as this will save the kings reputation. It shall hold our kingdom together at these uncertain times."

"What has happened here! How has he bewitched you?"

"Liam, do not speak ill of your father..."

"I'll speak of how he's been treating you! He abuses you both verbally and physically. Why, It is against your honor! Treated in this fashion and mine for what you ask of me. Can't you see mother in the state of mind that he's in, it won't be long before there is a next time."

My mother looks on as if in a daze. I continue to confront her pains; as I sense fear be upon her.

"He's broken your spine! What'll he break next? He's got to be stopped!"

"The kingdom is at the verge of war. We must stand by your father!"

"Are we to stick by him by aiding in his illness?"

Something is not right within me, I find my soul starting to thirst and turn away. The Spirit of the Great

One from the words of the pattern in the *Book of Life*; it causes me to recall the past few times I'd been around my father.

It hits me! I realize that I had lost a part of me every time I saw father and it is now my mother who has become the reflection of his image. *"What I am relating with here is more than fear, it's a lie!"*

I look back towards my mother, who has become 'the queen' in my eyes.

Then seeing the greater truth, one who is the Hierarchy of a greater worth than royalty, I speak freely.

"You dishonor yourself when you side against the truth, and bring dishonor against our kingdom. What appears, as innocence, within the pattern of your thoughts 'your majesty' will eventually put out light for us all.

For this lie is a base for evil to fester and bring disorder to our subjects."

"I'll not be addressed in such a manner..."

"In such a manner? Turn your back on the righteousness of our Great One and you'll march over the cliff into an abyss. For no longer will you have His light to guide.

As for me, locked away in some dark lie, imprisoned within my soul I'd be; for the rest of my life.

Among the priests I have tasted truth. I have read from the *Book of Life*, and now have light to see with balance in soundness of mind; which you are trying to suppress!"

My emotions start to well up inside; my voice breaks from the sadness of this situation, as I continue,

"I would be unable to be who I truly am and you my queen would not escape the stench of this foul lie either."

I sober up and stand with my hands at my sides before her, "You'll lose sight of the truth, your love, and then you'll lose all light. Why, your life will lose meaning and you'll wander about as ghost. Lost you will be; until the true value of your 'Royalty' will become cheap imitation..."

"The king has given His command!"

"I'll go to the proconsul. They'll know the truth is a command that can overrule any lie."

"They already know and are anticipating your signed confession."

"I see a lot has happened here since the priests have left. However, I will not pay with my soul by succumbing to these fears.

As, within my new self worth I see that I now have. There is love for who I've become. Don't tell me that you don't know that compromise is too high a price to pay!"

"No one will believe you Liam; they'll be strong consideration that you're the one who's lying."

"I never would have believed it of my own mother. To hear my father's words of deceit and treachery coming out of your mouth. What has happened to our family?"

"Liam, it is the only way I now know."

I find myself looking at my queen in her discontentment and have compassion, as we both start to weep.

Moved, I embrace her again, but this time there is warmth between us. My queen, once more becomes my mother. "Don't trouble yourself; the Great One is in control here. A plan has been revealed that will help father..."

My mother looks up with a glow upon her face, "I wish that I had faith like you."

"Have faith the size of a mustard seed and you can say to a mountain get up and be cast into the sea. Now, seeing the Great One has given you new desire, set up a meeting between me and father!"

She looks at me with a pause, "I'll see. Let's see what the Great One will do."

"Mother, it has to be a public meeting as father has threatened me."

"I understand."

"I'll be by the drinking pool in town at around eleven in the morn on the morrow."

"I'll speak to your father."

X

Taking leave through the passageway, I begin groaning in my spirit.

Remembering the closeness I had with the brethren, I long for their fellowship.

I stop, brace my arm against a wall, and let my thoughts come; grasping to understand them.

In reflection, there was something about the bond we shared at the monastery. *"It was beyond an intimate nature, where all was brought to the depths of love in reality; such great affection within our love for the truth. Why, it was greater than all else; contentment was found!"*

Now I see, even at this distance we're joined together; I sense it is by their prayers.

Next, it hits me. *"If I bear witness of the truth itself, which doth not change, then the Great One shall speak directly through me to father; as with the viper at the watering hole when leading my horse."*

It's further revealed, how the countenance changed on mother through my words and embrace. *"I've been kept away too long, too much has dimmed the Great One's light."* I then conclude, *"I am armed with understanding!"*

Oh, my father in his glory days; full of life. I know we shall have him back again. Even in the face of this affliction from that accursed witch; who has him all but gone. I see how her darkness has brought a complacent apathy to father, leaving a boredom to escape by way of drink. I know evil yet attacks his mind, and not only harms his soul, but all those who are around Him.

This touch of evil has affected the lives of so many. It seems now that these days will never end.

"Yet, my confidence is in You Oh Great One. There shall be joy throughout Calington once again; even the same joy that You have given me."

It is the center of town, merchants are busy trading at the square. Near the center of its plaza there is a large open drinking pool.

Slabs of rock have been laid round about the water, as buffer when the winds kick up dust. Granting easier access to draw a drink is yet another purpose for these stones.

I arrive with my hood up, as to not be recognized. Being a little warm under my robe, I sit on one of the slabs of cool stone by the water. From here, I watch the busyness of the merchants.

Now, my thoughts take me back to the visit I had with mother in another light. I take notice that there was a spirit behind my mother; trying to have me play its role that would cater to the lie of a seduction. Yet, when I stood in the Great One's might, my true love for Him overcame the captivity of this evil.

I'm going over the many blessings of the Great One in my mind when the strong fragrance of a young maiden's perfume suddenly captures my attention. I find myself watching her, as she passes by. Strangely, I'm drawn to her beauty. She looks back towards me and I catch myself watching; I know what is happening to me.

"Why is there such a yearning within my soul to have her? Am I not a priest who looks to be fulfilled by the Great One? Is not He able to meet all my needs?"

I question my mind, but my heart still has longings that I've yet to understand. I know I cannot satisfy spiritual things with fleshly desires. Though, I must be led of the right Spirit to clearly see who be right for me.

"Oh Great One, I know you are able to meet my needs. Deliver me during this time of affliction. Help me to be still and fly away with You in the midst of my storm; 'til Your love has hold of my heart much more!"

I remember innocence of youth. How, washed and dressed, with hair brushed; so many instructors shaping my mind. *"So much care, why, even then 'My Great One' were You not there?"*

I can't say, How I remembered when I preferred to do most things for myself, but they were stepping stones towards being a man.

Now, here lay, another stepping stone. I am to confront her spirit with a passion that has turned my heart towards true compassion. *"I see that she too has fallen into a pit; which she cannot climb out."*

It is quickened, the same way I am to confront the dragon jailer who has locked hold on her. The king's heart shall be freed; the Great One shall restore him to being father again.

He will be released, by the sword of light, from this one who lurks around in the same shadows; bypassing his imprisoned soul, as likened unto her. She shall bear witness of exit from sin, just as darkness will leave my father's soul.

For within my observation of the way my father's been treating everyone lately, it is a sure sign he too has an evil presence. I must wait for the proper time, but could this be it?

As a child others shared their faith with me, but now, am I really ready for something more? Wait, I am forgetting something that I should know to remember, something about the time I spent at the monastery or even how the dragon was defeated in the valley?

It is then decided by divine desire, *"I must experience a relationship with the Great One in this area of my life as well. It is time to learn more of the knowledge of His grace first hand."* The same maiden passes a second time, but by the presence of the Great One I've become more aware of her pattern.

A little more growth, come into focus, gives a more complete image of Him. I'm being flirted with, because I'm wearing the chaste robe of a priest, and this is evil.

I continue to see that suffering happens where love and truth are hindered from coming together. For, all is thrown off-balance. Now, there is sight in this moment as well.

There's a process in the formation of light. Where, calling on the Great One, understanding comes to bring order. This is what directs our choice to stop all darkened plights. As Better vision allows us sight to see Him clearly. For love burns deeper within my heart. I'm lifted out of all that held me to the dark.

I discern this maiden to have a false base of malcontent; built upon by one disappointment after another. The poor maiden has the eyes of one that is about to give birth to a dragon.

"Oh Great One, help this one, have mercy upon her soul. Set her free from suffering the darkness of angry blinding bars of stone. I see she has reached a place in her life where she is ready for change. So I place her in your faithful hands."

After sharing the intent of my heart in this public place. I watch, as truth from prayer bears witness of it-self. The maiden starts to weep before coming to a pause, then kneeling before me with her head down. I say unto her, "Child, arise."

Slowly, rising to reveal herself. She lifts her head, but now with a wide smile and tears of joy.

"The Great One is with you-go in peace."

Continuing to smile she nods her head in recognition, with a brand new look in her eyes, quietly she goes on her way.

I am still now. The Great One's confidence now rests within the quiet of my soul. The *Book of Life* then comes to mind," but before I can reach into my robe to take it out sounds of trumpets divert my attention.

It is fan fair for the king that suddenly breaks my focus. I then realize that my wait is over. He has come, my father has come. Now I will know the Great One here as well. I wait, watching in anticipation, as to what will next unfold?

Proclamation then goes forth, "Make way! His Majesty King Henry visits the market place."

My father dismounts his horse and walks by a few shops accompanied by his guard; his subjects bow as he passes.

After completing his entrance my father relieves his personal guard and walks towards me; sitting by the well. A thought from the Great One then reminds, how much I love the beauty of His living truth, which grants full joy in the freedom of His peace. It is known above all else. For I know I have been set free by Him.

My father draws water from one of many clay cups that reside on the slabs of stone. He takes a drink, turns, and speaks gruffly to me. "I believe we have a meeting."

"Father I have missed you."

"And I you, now let's hear what's to be said and be quick about it!"

I compare my countenance, which I had with the priests to that of his majesty's now fast paced presence. *"I am tempted to sway to the terror of his unruly authority.*

Yet, rather than be moved towards his spirit of contention, as he threatens the character of my stability. I remain still."

I have chosen to stand within the Great One's pattern of rest and all else yields to His protection. Repelling what is evil, joined to His peaceful presence, I am found within the safety of His fortress. Now a confidence that is not of my own next speaks through me in Spirit and in truth.

"Father, it is of the utmost importance to your family, your kingdom, and to your enemies that your honor be upheld."

"My honor? What's wrong with my honor?"

"Your actions are hurting all those around you and our subjects are becoming divided. The people do not feel safe around you anymore. They're starting to back away from your voice, which holds our kingdom together so well."

"So what would you suggest Liam?"

"If you were to admit before the kingdom that you struck mother, and are powerless to change. You'd leave room for the Great One to be the confidence of not only your life, but all who have been faltering.

For with Him to meet your needs your life would shine for us again. So brightly would it shine that our enemies would flee due to the brightness of your integrity, as the unity of our subjects would be strengthened. There'd be no more room for darkness either; it would not be there to allow spirits to afflict again."

"Ahhhg! This is all nonsense. I have always ruled well. Your' not obeying me is what is out of order here. Is that clear?"

I see that my knowledge is pushing away the king from knowing the affections of my heart.

"Father, you know I love you. You can trust my voice. Know, there is a role that goes with your position. If you call to remembrance, your role is to uphold the truth, which reveals all.

Do otherwise, and as one who has fallen from a position of balance, you shall denounce your kingship. Wherein this situation, it is my observation, you'll hate everyone around you in the end. For love will not be present within the dark."

"I am king here!"

"And I must honor the higher calling when your order tells me your behavior is contrary to the truth! My love for you be true; what's been happening here has been a painful time for all. Keep acting this way and no one will want to be around you anymore.

In a fit of rage the King suddenly pushes me to the ground.

'Please! I beg you father—don't make things worse; continue on your present path and we may even lose the kingdom.'"

"You've been with those priests haven't you?"

"I've been with the Great One Himself, whom man and king a like do bow before."

My father and king without even a nod in my direction looks away calling to his messenger, "Quill and parchment!"

He fumbles a bit, as he approaches, but then quickly hands them over to my father with the addition of a small container of ink. I watch as he coldly pens out a message in military fashion.

This can't be happening; I've got to do something to stop this isolation between me and him, so I speak my mind. "You're not my father, you're not my king, you're an imposture! I wager you don't even remember how we used to spend time together.

Name something we did together in the past and prove me wrong."

My father raises his wrist to his forehead, with quill still in hand, it appears as though his darkness is weakening.

Then I remember something that the Monsignor said, *"Good loving memories will help fight the spirits behind the spell. For the power behind evil is a lie and will cave way to the greater love of that which is true."*

"Oh father, why can't we go hunting like we used to and forget about formalities; remember the hikes we used to take in the mountains during the heat of summer. I wish we could be alone again, just you and me."

"I need a drink! Where's my golden goblet?" I watch a servant bring his cup and fill it. Father takes a long hard drink, and with wine still running down his face he returns it saying, "Fill it again!"

A stroke here, a stroke there, with the letter now finished he hands the parchment, quill and ink, back to his messenger. The king then motions for there to be more fan fair.

I can feel my heart beating within my chest, and try to pray, but before the trumpet stops I suddenly feel compelled to wait upon The Great One.

This is when I see the maid who I had prayed for earlier; horse in hand. She motions to me and I follow her lead, as the messenger reads "Here ye, Here ye. King Henry gives proclamation." The people stop what they are doing and gather, as I slip through them. "Let it be known that Prince Liam has struck the queen and has just now returned to make public apology.

I mount up upon hearing the proclamation. Somehow, I next ride away without even being noticed. The realization then comes, "The Great One has just delivered me."

Inside the monastery everyone is going about their daily chores. A knocking comes from the front. It continues to echo throughout the complex.

James puts down his hoe before a slowly setting sun in the garden and finds his way to the alcove. Then passing the smaller floral garden at its front. He anticipates a possible passing traveler.

The knocking continues and approaching the open area before the doors, I watch as his face lights with excitement upon opening unto me.

He then cries out to the others, "It is Prince Liam!"

We next embrace with warm affection, and everyone gathers round in a welcoming way. In the complex I drink in all their affirmations of love. I am with the brethren again, and it feels good to be accepted for me being me, after the fall out I had with father.

Then something more pressing, I can no longer keep to myself, comes to mind. It breaks from beneath the surface, letting out what troubles my heart I make it known.

"Brothers!" Everyone quiets down to give ear to what I have to say.

"I come to you on the account of corruption in the castle! I must share what is upon my heart. As I know I am amongst family. I value your opinion on what's to be said."

Noticing their attentive expressions I continue.

"The king has broken from his position of balance and no longer upholds the light of truth. He has blamed me for his corruption, having darkness, before all of Calington."

There are some gasps. I hear the word treason buzz around and then John speaks out, "You will stay with us 'til we are united on this matter."

Matthew, adds. "'Remember you not Liam's character?' Now, I say we pray that we'll not enter into judgment. So be not moved from your position of peace of the Great One's love or we'll be hindered in our affection towards others."

I then proclaim, "You all know my father is under the influence of the golden goblet. We must pray for direction, as I was just with him. I know that outside of prayer he is beyond all reason at this point. I truly feel I have the will of the Great One on this matter.

So I need you to stand with me, as I'll confront the King before all of Calington. He dare not call the Great One's church a liar before the people." A mild mannered Peter speaks out, "I would like to hear a little more of the past events, leading to this matter. Then, after seeing what kind of pattern unfolds. I will be better able to discern if we're to stand united."

I agree and tell them of the events that have taken place since my departure over dinner. Unanimously, they agree to come with me and that we should pack at once; for the cool night would be a kinder march than the heat of the day.

It seems evident, we are meeting within the Great One's timing. For everything is so quickly falling into place.

"Great One, I am afraid of what is yet to come. I fear for the lives of the brethren. Help us in this time of need, as I am yet a child in the understanding of Your ways."

I find all eyes suddenly be upon me, as I've just prayed aloud without even realizing it. Then, James, John, Peter, Matthew, and all the rest of the brethren move into fight out the battle in corporate prayer, but I find a more pressing need for something else. Quietly, I slip away.

Walking through the corridors I start to collect my thoughts. *"When I first read from the Book of Life everything seemed so clear. Now everything seems to be coming a part. Found to be alone in the midst of what's going on, even though surrounded by the brethren. 'How can I be sure of anything?'*

'Why, I'll again read from the Book of Life!'"

I find my way to my bunk and make myself comfortable.

While reading the brethren come to mind. I next start to sense that I am no longer alone. Just then, I hear footsteps in the dorm quietly approaching.

I'm discovered reading by the Monsignor so I turn towards him, "How doth one know when to be sure?"

The Monsignor gives answer, "Sometimes, you just have to go by the faith that has been given you. Do you trust that the words from the *Book of Life* bear witness of the kingdom they are from?"

I ponder my thoughts for a moment or two, "Why, yes I do."

"Then the character of the Great One will balance out the rest. For even when we are faithless He remains consistent in the sacrifice of his faithfulness."

I look up from where I'd been reading. "I now see that there's no need for worry. As life without truth has no consistency. For, unstable in nature, it always produces a base of unbalance; forever unfolding to reveal instabilities of sickness. All within falsehood displayed as dark and hollow inside a mind.

Why, there is torment for all who build here. For they always suffer the weight of their house without a solid grasp of reality; wherein it keeps caving in upon them."

"In the balance of this very light, Liam. You are carried even from death to see with surest of sight. For wherever heaven and earth are joined together, during our darkest strife, truth will always bear witness of this or any weight being lifted. Just as our souls are restored from the words of love you now read. By His flesh He dwells among us and this is where all healing takes place.

For once the hold of blinding shadows be removed. They bring not sickness any longer. Valley's had steered us towards minds filled with night, but these thoughts are removed, when come into sight, and so to all fright."

"Monsignor, I know that the Great One's structure holds the deep mysteries of reality. For, by Him, we learn absolute consistency holds together all. He brings forth what is alive, and each day our ways are replaced from what had us bound with greater life.

I"m even discovering Him to walk, as one with grace, the way He gives us gifts. For from what you say, He's found within the substance of His pattern of sacrifice. One of which is still more than I know, as this vision yet escapes my growing revelations of light."

"I've found Him not even to address darkness within His pattern myself, if this might be a help. Rather He stands, as the light, so others be guided to find their way; then comes His stability of truth. So all may know where to find freedom while mending from the torments of suffering."

"Then it is He who must keep me content from within. It is His Spirit who loves and protects our lives; as what has depth in reality is training my eyes.

Plainly it must be seen. There's no place left open for other spirits to enter and steal our light when understanding His fulfilling grace is the plan of His purpose for life."

"We find our purpose Prince Liam, while learning our service to the Great One from the motivation of His love towards us. This is where sanity sparks desires to become fulfilled in Him. As words of prayer find their way beyond thin air. They enter, and touch, the bosom of His heart; when felt by what you know of His character."

"Then I am not to abstain from sin by loving me, as within self preservation, but rather to learn of His greater love; whereby joining myself to the Great One's mercy to bring deliverance. I see now that in love there's always the learning of what was paid for me by sacrifice. How this draws me even closer to Him."

"His light Liam, guides through distress. For by His names sake, calling upon Him my needs are met. He has a distinct voice and found am I on His path of delights. For listening to His living words from the *Book of Life* leads not only me, but all to rest–and here I too am content."

"I now know how to ask for His love in time of need. As I too identify with Him. He has the strength to replace my sight.

For His timing allows all to behold Him as right. When seen here He meets me, and I know what it is to hold Him that much more; enough to bring me out of any dark pit. Wherein looking to find favor, in everything I do, instead I am translated before Him; as out of love everything is new.

Attacked by dragons yet I'll be, but not to dismay; there be no chains that can bind my mind anymore. My mission is now to find His loving authority, and call upon Him to do battle against them."

"Yes!"

"My father was the stabilizing force in my life. I see now that the Great One's been there all along, waiting for me to come to Him, while holding all my pieces in place for me."

"Be aware of the grace of this answer Liam, as the presence of His established base now rests within you. Your focus has changed to become like Him. Why, He even yet continues to sew you into His heavenly pattern; build you upon His sure foundation."

"I must! I am to continue to experience His promise of abundant life, as better than what I have known. For He has given me light to better understand myself in the midst of any darkness; even before I first began my journey with Him."

"Are you ready to join the others Prince Liam, or is there still something that prevents us from moving within the Great One's timing?"

"A patient thought then tells me: the Great One gave His life in place of mine that I may have a true royal worth."

"Prince Liam?"

I do not want to answer. *"I want my Lords words to enhance my new identity in full embrace. His Spirit lets His words craft me, more unto His likeness, as they slowly sink in.*

In His new image I'm being liberated by grace upon glorious grace. Where I've discovered Him to actually enter into the fibers of my flesh."

"Monsignor, my mind and heart have come together in agreement. A full revelation appreciation within the beauty of His gift of light has raised me up.

Praise be to the Great One, for it is by His grace that all I now have is faith in Him; I am ready."

"Are you sure you're ready perhaps you need more time?"

"Monsignor, If you feel uneasy about this trip, you may remain behind."

"No, most assuredly, I am His servant too. I am with you!"

We are 120 priests in the Great Ones strength marching out into the night towards Calington.

Some of the other brethren remain behind, as they have house duties to tend to in their turn of the rotation. All are equally important on this quest. For with a base to stem out everything is held in place. As the history of the *Book of Life* would only be as scattered leaves if not for its root, which all draw from. This is the Great One's sacrifice, giving purpose to all who join this new vine. Where pages, as leaves, sprout the living Spirit of Life.

There are two pack mules that walk in our midst; they carry food in addition to extra water. Although there are horses there are not enough for us all, so I opt not to ride.

Besides, I prefer walking amongst the company of my brothers. As this allows more time to share our common loving bond; which to me is of a greater value.

Afterwards, there are good feelings in the air, my mind grows even sharper from our cause. Sight of clarity recognizes a mutual acceptance, as I am humbled by my walk with them.

We are all led by two brothers who bear lanterns tied upon walking staffs before a less than half moon. Not too far behind them, myself and the Monsignor are walking side by side.

We are all in agreement while walking. I sense unity of love is within the truth of this 'peace.' Where inside containing a part of this kingdom, each contribute, as we now bear strength by having our own place. A testimony of witness bringing harvest complete. For, when walking in the Great One's existence, contentment be found.

The sounds of crickets are heard all around and this encourages me in song. Words well up within my soul, and I sing them out:

"Be aware...that He is near, holding all together in its place. He holds my heart, just right you know. He keeps me warm by His loves embrace. The way is lit, for all to come. So join in my joy, for freedoms march...all of the way to Calington."

Upon hearing my song the brethren join in, which leads to more singing with other songs of further encouragement. Though all surroundings are black, it seems to me there is much more light present than that of the lanterns, which aluminate our way.

I can taste the dust from the road, as it is kicked up from under our feet by the stillness of the air. This is no dream, although it is night, we are marching for what is real.

In between conversation with the Monsignor, when all is quiet, the Great One's fire burns to satisfy my desire. Held am I within position, from everlasting love, lit inside my heart.

I wonder about my mother, which leads me to pray for father. Then my mind wanders as to how Edward is yet doing too. I laugh at the thought of how he will respond to me being the deliverer. I do miss him so.

The light of first morn peels back the darkness of the night. We all remain strong and continue to march.

The lantern bearers douse their lights; falling in line after fastening their staffs and lanterns to the mules. There is such peace when everyone knows their place. For there is purpose in the heart when the reward of order is great.

Soon morn falls way and we find ourselves facing an afternoon sun. I take a drink from one of my skins and upon seeing a grove of some rather large trees up ahead; we all agree to take refuge under their shade.

No one complains, not a word of discord, for we all know that our mission is in the Great One's timing, and for this reason its taste is sweet.

After disbursing some provisions from the mules, we give thanks and take eat. I find a comfortable place upon having satisfied my flesh. Now leaning against one of the trees I open the *Book of Life* and start to read to satisfy my spirit as well. The Monsignor comes over.

"It's good to see you reading my prince, but why don't you get some rest."

"Being with all of you has helped me to understand that you get to know a person a little at a time; this is why I must be read this book a little each day. As I'm now ready to join Him completely in His story!"

"Well spoken majesty. I've given instructions for the first to wake from His nap to arouse the others; so that we might be on our way again. As you can see the mules have been tied..."

"Post a watch."

"That won't be necessary for this trip, for I have prayed."

"...There could be bandits in these parts who might have taken in some bad counsel, from other preachers, and may have offense with us before we open our mouths."

"It is your old military nature that speaks. Why, to do so will break confidence of trust with the Great One."

"The *Book of Life* says, "It rains on the just and the unjust." Aren't these the words of the Great One too?"

"I will post a watch your majesty."

"The sentry can rest on one of the mules when we continue our march."

"Understood."

All is quiet now that we've settled down, but in this stillness I've become more sensitive; sensitive to the fact that there may be disunity in the oneness of the body of believers on this march.

Then the thought comes to mind, 'There's a traitor among us!' I start to go over in my mind, who? Yet, I can't quite shake the feeling that a spirit other than the Great One watches over us.

"Curse you Prince Liam and your watch!"

The witch that had sent me to my doom, in the valley of the dragon, watches over us by the spirits of her crystal.

Shacha, the king of Orth is being persistent in his impatience, "Well, what have you come up with?"

"This prince is more than resourceful to have defeated my dragon. He has been more familiar, with use of sword of Spirit, by the Great One's light than I had thought; so now I must finish him off before he gets me. Let's see how He will fair without weapons against the Orthian swords of steel."

"Now that's my kind of language!"

It is suddenly quickened to my mind that a guard has never been posted.

I spring to my feet and from the look of the sun; it hangs around three o'clock in the sky. We have slept about four hours. I look over to the Monsignor who stumbles to His feet.

"I thought I said to post a watch!"

"I am that watch!"

"You were asleep when I arose."

"The same spirit that has awakened you has quickened me too." I hear noise in the brush coming steadily towards us.

"Awaken everyone we are under attack!"

The Monsignor's eyes lock with mine, "Traitor!"

"It was a test to see if you really are the deliverer."

"Why have you betrayed us? It is written 'You shall not put the Great One's Spirit to the test!'"

They break from the tall grass with drawn sabers; shining in reflection of the sun. I see them from off in the distance.

I take note of their spirit and see their dark countenances. In an instant I recognize that there is no place for truth to be found among them.

I then shout, "Prayer circle!"

The priests quickly fall in line to form a circle, and we join one another's hands.

The Monsignor goes to join in, but we forbid him; for he has lied and joined in with the worship of darkness.

"If you're telling the truth, and have compassion in your heart, you have nothing to fear."

Sobering up, he quickly comes to his senses, "Hear me everyone! The witch has my niece and threatens to kill her. I had to follow what she requested of me. Some Orthians stole her away during the cover of night—It was before our March!

My guess is that when they saw they could not get at you Prince Liam, they took Ashley. I have a note back at the monastery that explains all.

The witch is merciless, with that seeing crystal of hers, she has me under her grinding thumb and knows my every move.

I was only to delay you. I knew nothing of an attack, you have my word!"

"Evil strikes at our weakest point that the Great One can strengthen us where we're found unprepared."

The Monsignor asks for our forgiveness with tears running down his face. He then confides on how he has missed being a part of the unity of the brethren, and the merciful grace of our compassionate Great One.

"You know my heart loves! How could I have jeopardized your lives?" Discerning his Spirit I'm moved with compassion. "Even now you've been forgiven, come quickly, stand in our weaknesses that the power of our Great One's grace be perfected here as well. I want you to trust that Ashley will be protected, as we face this enemy!"

The Orthians have murder written within their hearts. For destruction shows forth darkly, as seen in their eyes. I see only madness upon their face, as they advance, but for no other reason than to take our lives.

With a rushing mighty wind our hearts are joined in one accord; I then pray for us all. "Oh Great One, I have no desire to see our enemies suffer. Please grant them the grace of knowing You, and if it be within thy will to live, protect us. 'Your children' call upon none other than You. Grant that no harm shall come to the Monsignor's niece as well!"

My palms suddenly become hot as an invisible wall of fire encircles us. "I sense the Lords presence is here to protect." We all then call to the Orthians to respect our persons that they may live, but they choose to continue in their disrespect. They advance, as if death had no meaning.

Being under a curse, by their own choice, they do not heed our warning and advance until consumed by the grace of our Lord's protection. It is an invisible wall of flame they meet 'til only their ashes remain.

"It is a fearful thing to fall into the hands of a living God," then comes to mind; quickened from the words of the *Book of Life*.

While still in our positions, we are all left standing in awe. Many mercies are realized as thanksgivings go up. Being allowed to comprehend His power, all hands are in the air.

Even so, we've still yet to fathom to greater extent this one drop in the vast sea of grace which now refreshes our minds.

XI

The witch is in a frenzy, as she paces back and forth in front of her crystal ball. After the destruction of the Orthian assassins, she's at a loss for what next to do.

"He cannot be seduced, he already has wealth, the Great One protects Him from all physical harm, spiritually he discerns, and now he has the *Book of Life*. If I cannot beat him I may have to join him."

She comes to a pause as her eye's open wide.

"Wait! the *Book of Life*, I'll attack him through his thoughts with my version of verse from the *Book of Life*.

Hmmm! I don't think he's Knowledgeable enough yet to know that truth doth not hang on any one verse, rather than the whole testimony of the book.

Let's see now, how can I twist Prince Liam's faith best? 'Faith without works is death', mixed with the thought, 'It's upon him to honor the Great One with self effort according to the pretense of a false context–that should do for a start."

Spirits of the wind I call you up!"

The witch, walking quickly around the room, encircles the crystal ball before her. She then raises her arms as though she is lifting something within the palms of her hands. She continues to call upon the wind, 'til a dark cloud appears over her crystal sphere.

"Doctrine of demons severed from root of vine... spirits of wind! I command you to carry and deliver these thoughts I have placed in my crystal to the mind of Prince Liam, now!"

The witch then turns to an Orthian sentry and sends for the niece of the Monsignor.

When summoned, Ashley is allowed to walk freely to meet this woman of darkness. As her uncle has explained to her that this is who the witch really is. She enters the room.

"Come and join us Ashley; have some cake and we will have a most special little visit."

"My uncle has told me about you! You oppose the truth of the Great One; who is kind and gentle, patient and loving. I'll not have any part with you!"

"Is that fair? You're not being very patient with me right now. Why, you've not even heard a word of what I have to say."

Ashley, takes a deep breath; slowly she lets it out, but not towards the Great One. Then thoughts come to her mind of how she can probably handle the words of this witch on her own,

"All right, let's hear it."

"Too much structure, not enough freedom, don't you want to do whatever you want, whenever you want to? Isn't this what everyone desires? Faith like a child, isn't this what you need to enter heaven?

Don't you remember the freedom you had when you were younger? How you ran like the wind!

Well I'm still running, come and join me?"

The words of the witch start to become more vivid than having faith in the Great One, as she continues.

"The Great One wants us to be confined; this is what is evil. We have our rights. I will not be confined!

Why don't you come and join me Ashley?

Imagine how much fun we could have in the freedom of running together.

I will teach you how to have spirits do your biding for you, for whatever you desire–

Perhaps a nice prince to serve you?"

Ashley, is suddenly quickened by the Great One's Spirit and responds: "You want me to have a controlling relationship, within manipulative–apathetic–complacency. Where people use and abuse each other, within patterns of hate and lust in place of a genuine love having stability. This only leads to shared insanity!

Why, with myself in control, without respect, I'd be controlled by the darkest spirit of all.

Juggling the universe 'til its weight came crashing down upon me; slowly crushing me to death in madness!

Maybe that's your best choice, but I know in whom I believe. Word became flesh and dwelling among us; line upon line. He's the one whose built into the whole of my being by His pages of life. Seeing how there's nothing to protect me, without Him, knowing your lying roots. Now I see your world is dying.

For joined to deep reality itself, and connected inside Him, above the shallows of what you say. My sight tells me you are being swept away!"

"What a dull imagination your uncle has given you! I will help you to go back to where this damage was done. If you'd put your trust in me to guide you in the right direction.

For it pleases me to leave the beauty of my power to someone just like you, what do you say about that Ashley?"

"You cannot go back once having truly tasted the weightier affirmations of love. I'll not settle for second best when I've the pearl of greater life.

For there is no turning back to being isolated, unless the Great One's structure is used to stir memories to suit His purposes of passionate prayer; needed to have compassion for others.

I tell you. This is where order need be or everything held by the Great One would dry out. Then, in times of drought, due to a lack of our Lord's Spirit. We would break away from His branch like a twig on a windy day; except for mercy, why only damage would be incurred.

Besides? What kind of trust would I have otherwise? As the power behind your counsel would suggest stability with uncertainties, and this is deception!

Life is about growth and going forward. You can take hold of any old roots if you wish, but your desires will lead nowhere! For they have no depth, while on a base that is changing, leaving malcontent."

The witch seemingly intrigued with the way she has responded inquires of her further, "What about the Great One doth He change?"

"You know better than I! For it is in His perfection, which cannot change, you steal your power; out of envy for sorcery.

From the same origin we were initially created! Why are you trying to trap me?

As you know there is no order without structure. No room to have freedom for greater selection, when out of control, as reality remains shallow without foundation and one cannot grow.

There's no truth for control to choose freely apart from the stability of a firm foundation. I'll not be compliant to suit your purposes; as you want me to be defiant against the order of love, structured in truth, so I cannot have balance in sight. Thus will I do myself harm and those around me. For as structure becomes displaced, your world of darkness can truly come in and invade.

After seeing you and knowing my uncle, I now understand the verse from the *Book of Life*.

'You will know the truth and the truth will set you free,' and I choose to continue building only upon it. For in seeing you have called what is real and good evil, and what is evil in falsehood good. Your depraved comparisons make all stale.

In seeing this, I am humbled to be back on His path again."

The witch then seems to sound like she is softening for a moment. "I'd like to tell you a story about your mother."

"I know who both my mother and father are, as revealed to me by The Great One Himself. I'll hear no more from your dark tongue!"

"Silence her at once!"

The sentry draws his sword and advances on Ashley who is standing full of faith.

When the sentry swings his sword, it is him and not Ashley who meets his fate, turning to ash his remains hit the floor.

The witch's mouth drops open.

She then remembers the prayer of Prince Liam for the Monsignor's niece and priests. "Liam must be the deliverer!"

Ashley, turns to the witch. "Why don't you come with me, take my hand?"

"Where do you think you are going!"

"I feel sorry for you."

The witch quickly examines her thoughts, *"If I take her hand, as a free will offering, maybe I can ring her neck. Yet, the Great One's Spirit may be upon her; then I too would be a pile of ash upon the floor if I were wrong!"*

She next tries to bluff her way through, "You can't leave; orders have been given for your destruction!"

"You can kill my body, but never will my soul be imprisoned. For, long after I'm gone, you will still feel the weight of your own...Eternally imprisoned choice. How do you expect to escape the sting of death?"

The witch freezes in the light of what has just been said; Ashley then sees it in her eyes, "You've been nothing but a liar! I see plainly now I have had the power to leave all the time. For the Great One's shield of faith protects me."

Ashley, turns to leave. On her way out she hears the witch say in a feeble voice, "Come back and visit an old woman when you can."

Having overcome all obstacles by the divine hand of the Great One. Ashley takes leave, as locked doors melt away. No spirit or man, outside of love and truth in balance, dares to cross her path. When last seen her destination was for that of Calington Castle.

XII

The Monsignor is speaking to me. Trying to bring up some point about the pace we are marching is too hard.

"Nonsense, we are being governed by the pace of the Spirit of the Great One. We've got to try our hardest in order to fulfill living up to the honor of our calling!"

"Now I know you are in error! We are not to be carried about by a strange compulsive doctrine. For it is good that the heart be established of an excellent peaceable Spirit by grace.

Majesty, by trying to get things done in your own timing, you are fueling your flesh that is at war with the Spirit."

"What proof do you have of this?"

"Look at the brethren, do we still move as one breath or is your breath leading ours into restlessness? Remember the oneness that we shared during the attack of the Orthians? Do we still stand in one mind and accord?"

"We Monsignor, could go on 'til meeting where the road turns by the big rock before Calington."

"It is not just rest that I am speaking of!

If we were to arrive without being prepared. We would be off balance, and bear a perception for disaster. We must share, the same pace of peace, within the Great One's pattern of clear sight before we go another step. As the distance within our ranks to move, as one, would cause a hindrance between us. For when distortions move in, bringing division to unity, they only create barriers."

"Look, it is the sign post to Orth! Calington is but a few hours from here!" The Monsignor motions to the brethren before sitting down with them. I continue to coax them on and somehow miss the message that the priests are giving me, "Its just a little further, can't you see we must get there!"

"Compulsion is not in accordance with the character of the Great One." The brethren then begin calling to me. They encourage me to sit with them, share in the love of His truth with balance, but I only grow worse.

A young maid is then heard from the road, "We love you Prince Liam!"

As her voice cries out; it is discovered to be that of Ashley.

The Monsignor's niece has just come off the road from Orth. Having overheard us she walks over in the Great One's timing.

The Monsignor, upon hearing her voice, throws his arms up in the air while dancing round and round in joyous circles, "Praise be to the Great One, I tell you He lives!"

All the brethren cheer as she approaches, "It was by your prayer Prince Liam, I escaped the witch. The Great

One's Spirit is yet upon me, and I have walked in the joy of His peace all the way here.

Take my hand; let us sit together amongst the brethren."

Ashley's piety I can in no way refuse, so I sit with her amongst our brothers.

Almost immediately I start to churn and wriggle about; my pattern has been altered by thoughts, which now differ from the brethren.

I feel trapped, separated, amongst those who love me. While darkly anguished, I let loose my mind that bubbles from beneath the surface of my soul.

"Day's without rest–day's without peace. Am I obsessed? Am I possessed, seeing this conflict. At first, it rises so slow, but then comes upon me swiftly. Why, there's a dragon in my head!"

There's no time for sight, as my thoughts are washed to and fro. "Who am I? Where am I? What am I to do, and where am I to go? I want to be obedient to love; am I being judgmental on the path I am now on?"

Within this battle, I'm met to feel the weight of confusion from my sin and am knocked off my high horse.

I next cry out after my prideful fall, "I need my peace! Where is my Prince of Peace?

Behold!

I see He is near, as now He is here."

I am stilled to enjoy my love's sweet embrace. "Great One it is You!

Your face I have sought, now once again–I see I've found Your mercy all by grace."

When I open my eyes I see a sea of faces reflecting my joy, which makes me all the more joyous.

I hear the Monsignor say, "The dark spirit has left him!"

Then we all shout together,

"Praise be to the Great One!" as one. I then add:

"It is only by the power of the Great One that I have risen!" We all have a feast of hugs, before walking off the main road to find some shade, and take in some much needed rest.

The next day, on the morn, we are back on the road again; this time all walking in one accord. The sun climbs in the sky, and having just rounded the turn past the big rock, I cry out. "Calington lay but just a few hundred yards ahead!"

I have called out to encourage the brethren in this long awaited moment; now within sight of all.

We all burn with the quiet love of the Great One in our hearts; partaking of the joy in each other's likeminded focus on our beloved.

Realizing the Great One is as much a part of the court of Calington, as within the throne room of my heart, all anticipation melts away.

I then announce to the brethren, as we're walking:

"It is far better spending time with the presence of the Great One, who appreciates you, than spending your substance with those who count your value as lesser worth.

Let us give glory to Him on this day; as it is He we send into battle before us.

It is He who has a timing to meet our every need. As He will lift the burden all share for Calington in this time of uncertainty in exchange for His faithful hand.

Be in like mindedness, rejoice and be within His timing. His grace is sufficient to maintain our stance upon level and holy ground; where the mountains have been made low and the valley's raised up, within a vision that clearly beholds our eyes.

Now, as led of what is purposed in our heart this day, let each one share it. For this warfare is not hand to hand combat, but against the ruler of the dark spirits that are found among the high places."

One at a time we take turns speaking out to further encourage each other, and our faith continues to bloom. Glorying in the light be our fight, and the Great One's banner is upheld outshining the sun. All other powers within shadow dark flee. For when disagreements are peeled away. His glorious throne of an all sufficient grace be revealed complete; right in evil's face.

In reality deep, we now begin to give testimony. For we all have had needs met, as purposed by the Spirit who has brought us closer together. Intimacy now rests upon us from the Great One Himself. Where once we had trouble resting from strife, which kept us from enjoying His affirmations. We are thrilled to enjoy an honest life; one without trying to earn approval from anyone.

All other spirits from our efforts step aside. Dragons tried to draw strength, but reflecting the Great One's Kingship, met with our testimonies, there is nowhere to hide.

He rests upon us. Light has opened our vision to their touch. We are where we're supposed to be. For the reality of His throne rests burning upon our hearts.

Our choice has become one with the Great One. For all have chosen what he has prepared in the way of life inside His timing.

In this moment our peace is guarded from doubt, and I listen, as my fellow soldier priests begin to give testimony on our march to the castle. I feast in the sweetest of tastes that now hold our confidence. As sharing in our Great Lord's Spirit, which is so good, in the prevalence of our likeminded lives; all rejoice on our march for Calington's freedom:

Malcolm, starts off. "I remember how life was tasteless, going through motions of living, everything was strife. Then the Great Shepherd got a hold of my heart. Leading to the meadow where grazing is good. Bearing moments now clearer from a satisfied mind; His voice is heard. As He is the river of joy that ever flows within waters of life."

Seth, then follows. "My best choices led me off the path of life. It is the Great One who is in control. This is the source from which all blessings flow, bearing witness to the character of true faith; for I know His path has sight."

Ashley, "I drink from the flow of His love, which now bubbles out of my heart to satisfy not only mine, but all souls I will encounter."

Bernard, "He has not brought us thus far for naught. He has each of us in our proper place, and will deliver victory into our hands."

Claude, "The Great One will not give us more than we can handle. He doth not leave nor forsake us during temptation!"

Platius, "Your love has been so powerful that it's penetrated my heart and set me in position."

John, "I have learned that a blessing is something that cannot be earned, but rather it is something that the Great One gives out of His love. So, being here is a blessing. Proving that we are very much loved."

Matthew, "When I sing praise, remembering my affections for the Great One, I am filled with intoxicating faith, and the right kind of Spirit."

Todius, "I have studied 'til His words became a part of me from within; now they are life."

Alumnous, "You must be stilled in order to be filled. I am overflowing with joy, as all else has been stripped away, and now His love allows me to guide others."

Cal, "I have learned to only share my faith when I'm questioned about my actions. For it is by prayer that I ask the Lord to fight my battles."

Levi, "I trust the Great One to reveal Himself in an even more unforgettable relationship, one where there continues to be no regrets. For He is as fresh bread taking the staleness out of life."

Paul, "I'm going forward thanking Him for each breath. Then when they grow long in the calm of His presence. I'll enjoy the Great One's company even more."

Lazarus, "His glorious truth broke the hardness of my heart, allowing His Spirit to bond me, with a full measure of life."

By the time we reach the castle we are more than encouraged. I'd even say that we are so drunk with joy, it allows for strength, which shakes us to our very core. Leading to believe we will find favor in whatever happens next.

As we're approaching the drawbridge across the field. There is an earthquake that shakes everything around us, but our peace continues to remain within.

At the Castle my father is drunk again. Still possessed with the wrong spirit; he has trouble dismounting his horse. He too shakes from the quake.

Then before all is said and done, with a drawn sword and confused, the king shouts at the wind; as though there is an invisible enemy.

My brother sees our father's dilemma and tries to aid him with much difficulty. Next, when the after shock hits from the quake, the horse suddenly rears and our king falls; landing on top of Edward.

My father staggers before gathering himself. He then commences to return his sword to its sheath. This is when he notices blood dripping from it. Next, seeing Edward's body, laying beside the horse, as if from a nightmare he cries out.

"Edward, my son! What have I done?"

Dropping to his knees, he raises his clenched fists to his forehead and continues to cry out.

"Help me! I'm losing my mind!"

A guard approaches and inquires, "Sire, what's wrong?" The king then shouts, "Get the royal healer!"

Upon seeing Prince Edward's lifeless body on the ground the guard responds, "At once your majesty!"

A crowd starts to form. The subjects look unto their weeping king who pulls his son into his lap. He holds him, as the guard takes leave.

Coming off the fields there's a feeling in the air that this earthquake has been a sign; all then agree, within the unity of the brethren, our Great One is with us.

An increase of faith breaks forth. We are easily permitted to enter the front gates that open, as if we've been expected. We step across the drawbridge.

There is no little confusion in the air of Calington; walking amongst the people arriving just after the quake. We take notice of the reactions on their faces, as though this were the end of the world.

Next, after seeing mouths drop open, a small commotion is spotted over by the stable. I notice a crowd of on lookers, taking in a view, with somber faces.

The brethren and I easily pass through the people; 'til before long I see my father and king crying. I realize there's been an accident when I see the healer by my brother's side.

The healer looks up from Edward's body with a look of despair on his face. Then I see the words roll from his lips, "He's gone."

Immediately; tears fill my eyes while in disbelief, but when I catch their salty flavor, as they trickle past my lips. I realize what has happened.

"No, Edward! No!"

Then something rises from inside me against my father. I know that murder is in my heart!

Just then, I see the priests at prayer and am reminded of where I belong. I go to them and receive many embraces; weeping uncontrollably. I then regain my senses, by finding the Great One's hand. I am quick to place it to my heart 'til only there is light. The Monsignor looks at me. "You're not the only one who weeps." He then looks to my father.

My anger melts and changes to compassion. For I am reminded by the right Spirit of who I've become.

Quietly, I kneel beside my father and place my hand on his shoulder, but to my surprise he recoils at my touch.

I respect his person and speak what is on my heart.

"Father, please let me in! We must be able to express our feelings otherwise we'll grow to further cut them off."

There is a long pause and although my father doth not respond, I can tell he listens.

"Do you still want to be distant from each other after all that has happened?"

My father groans aloud from his anguish. Leaning forward his crown starts to fall from his head; he then lets it drop to the ground. Pushing his hands through his hair he cries out. "Help me please, somebody help me!"

"Do you really want help father?"

He pauses from his grief while looking up at me; tears still roll down his face. "Liam, I do!"

Upon hearing my father's response I feel the tension break in the air. Yet, I sense a need to test his sincerity. In fact, I know I must see what has his heart.

"Father, my love is with you, but there is a pain that blocks my way from drawing near; even in the midst of our grief for Edward.

Can you understand that unstable thought leads to bad choices, always leaving us outside the treasure of how to love?"

I make it clear in so many words. If he humbles himself before the Great One's strength, by esteeming Him higher, all will be possible. "Liam, all is dark, what must I do?"

"First, you must set the record straight about our queen's accident. This is what will bring honor to your royal worth again."

The king pauses with a moment of silence; after weighing the choices that hang in the balance. A change then takes place, as he nods his head. Finally, surrendering to the truth of greater love, he now recognizes a bridge that need be crossed for us to bond. A look comes over him. It is as though he has found a treasure that was hidden; buried within a field.

"Yes, I must!"

The king then gathers himself, stands, and speaks out with an emotionally somber voice. His words break from his heart felt cords, which get caught in his throat.

He addresses his subjects who have gathered round.

"My subjects, and to those who are present from the court. Let it be made known this day I have struck the queen in drunken rage; it is because of me she doth not walk—and now the death of my son, over nothing!

I'm not even fit to be king anymore. Here Liam, take the crown and save the kingdom."

With all of Calington looking on, I ponder over how I am to answer. I am then overshadowed with wisdom from on high.

"No father, this is a part of being king. It is not my rightful time. For I have more to learn from you."

I hand my father back his crown and watch. He raises it, unsure, before slowly lowering it back upon his head.

A new found faith then comes upon him, as he shares: "It is the Great One who is the revealer of mysteries! I know that it is He who will save Calington, as I no longer desire to rule."

Seeing my father show genuine remorse. I open my arms to him and when we embrace a weight lifts from between us.

Celebration now fills the air, as the Great One's love touches the atmosphere.

The loyal subjects become heart warmed, as seen by the joyous expression on their faces. Now that honor is in the land again, smiles replace despair, truth prevails. I can see that the oppression has truly been lifted; order has been restored with our head now back in its proper place.

Looking through her crystal ball the witch has been watching all with King Shacha by her side. He starts to pace back and forth. "What do we do now that stability is back in their land?"

"If you'd hold still maybe you'd listen more intently. You forget the golden goblet. I will send forth a spirit to remind the king of how thirsty he is; when all has quieted down."

"No! Calington awakes from sleep. They now reflect, as one. That so called Great One's light. I see Him to keep away your spirits, as the king has confessed his lies.

He even now regains his strength within the kingdom's new light. Look how he has lit; especially since he has been around his son, which you let slip through our fingers."

"I have a plan, make ready your troops.

Now—that everyone's happy, their guards will be down. Oh my!"

"What is it?"

"All my evil thoughts are bringing me too much joy, ahhh hahh, ha, ha, ha.

Now, let me make the troops fearless by planting my special spirits of power upon their minds.

They should last through the invasion. Then I'll add more through my crystal, as needed.

I predict an easy victory!"

"I don't know how you do it, but again you have regained my confidence."

I call to my close brethren, "Father this is Luke, Matthew, James, John and Jerome." They are all aglow from the joy of the Lord...

"Andre and Louis you already know." The king still somewhat despondent greets them, and upon so doing, he finds his full strength return.

"Father it was their prayers and all the others that got us here."

"Monsignor, it has been a long time, I thank you for looking after my son."

"It is..."

"I know, all in the Great One's timing."

"Father, I want you to pray with us. I feel a stirring in my Spirit that the Great One will move."

We all join hands in agreement with one another and take turns in being led by the Spirit in prayer.

John, leads. "Oh Great One, hear us as thou always do. Heal our queen that she will walk. I know we shall see it and glorify thy name!"

Next, Luke joins in. "Lord the enemy troops have been on the advance. Before they reach our lines, let it be made known honor has been restored–and that our soldiers will be going forth in Your righteousness.

Even now, let our enemy be turned back that Your peace prevail!" Matthew, "I agree with my brothers. I too call upon You in accordance with Your Spirit. Oh Great One of living notes from the Spirit in the *Book of Life*. Keep our hearts open and continue to move on us, be our protector!"

James, enters the flow. "Oh Great One, during this time of uncertainty in Calington, I thank you for peace. Let it be our hearts song; that we will flourish to bring forth much life from Your current of love."

Finally, I share what is upon my heart, "I want us all to focus in on the Great One's gentleness as Creator.

'Oh Lord, my brother Edward lay dead. If thou art willing, I know that as thee living God of Creation, You can refashion my brother's flesh.

Hear my plea, heal his wounds and restore him unto life once more.'"

In accordance with the *Book of Life* I realize that He can actually do this. I release myself from the circle and slowly advance towards my brother's body.

"Edward, hear me. In the Name of our Great One who is King of all kings and sovereign Lord over all levels of heaven and earth.

Word become flesh, Almighty witness of sacrifice, foundation from all truth resting unshakable. Send back my brother, as You are the one who is the door between heaven and earth itself!

In the Name of Jesus Christ, the Nazarene, I say unto you 'Edward arise!" I am in awe that the Great One's name has just come from my lips. Still in the Spirit of gentleness everyone is in agreement that our Lord can do this.

I stop my advance before Edward, and my focus of faith cuts through the atmosphere.

"There is an anguish to uphold 'the truth,' but it be a lie. For it is grace, which shapes our lives, fulfilling all by His purpose; not merits of our own doing.

Loving Him is the power that has light! 'Your righteous sacrifice has lifted me; restoring all things.

You made me prince, priest, deliverer, and all who are alive live as royal kings. Your Name has fulfilled prophecy and made my conscious clear; that I'm able to know all within soundness of mind. For I can hear.

With merciful peace and loving grace, burning, as fire within my crying soul. I trust in You at depth of throne. I ask, by the power of Your redemptive blood, permit my brother to arise.'"

I look to my brother's body once again and then a vision comes to me; one of seeing things the way they are, as breath of life, even though not.

With seemingly feeble words I speak softly to him. "Edward, it is time to awaken."

As Edward awakes, his wounds close and he rises to his feet. "Oh, Liam when did you get here? I must have dosed off."

Before anyone can move, the queen walks into the courtyard and starts to leap joyously from the full use of her body.

"My son lives and my queen is restored!"

Father and I give hugs and kisses to Edward who is at a loss to understand why all the sudden affection, but when he notices all the blood on his clothes he recalls what happened.

"Wait a minute, that wonderful place–I was dead, yet I live, I'm back again! How is this possible Liam?"

"The Great One has been revealed as Jesus the Christ. Now many will find salvation in the completion of His Name, as His promise is fullness of life."

All give praise and adoration. There are many shouts with adornment to the glorification of God. Next, when all quiets down, the king's enthusiasm calms, astonishment causes him to take leave of his senses; he then questions, "What has happened here? How is all this possible?"

The next thing I know, I cannot believe what I see, my father is bowing at my feet. Why, while on his knees, he is worshiping me!

"Father, I am but a man of like passion as you."

I take him by the arm; raising him to his feet 'til meeting face to face. "Father, come back from the dimness of the dark, and remember the power of the living Lord; our life beyond Life. As the Great One has revealed His full Name to you.

In case you didn't hear, all these things have come to pass by Jesus who is the living Christ; savior to us all, as He is the promised seed to Abraham."

"I want to know our Jesus more fully again; even to know the brilliance of His face, as He is the One who is Great.

For in looking to you, I can see that the words from His book are alive. Most powerfully He has kept you at such peace; much more than I ever remember knowing than before. For in all of the storms I have put you through your love for me did not fail."

"Continue to receive His full Spirit of love, and you will always recognize his voice."

I watch, as my father and king walks over to the saddle bag on his horse. Quickly he opens it.

Next, bringing forth the golden goblet, he fumbles with it and drops it to the ground.

My father looks down at the cup calling for a cask to be brought.

"I propose a toast to Jesus, my Great One, whom I now see to shine, as reflected in the joy of all of you."

He then takes it and proceeds to pour out a good portion of wine upon the golden goblet in the dirt, and toss it.

"Now that I've found my Christ to be more beautiful, I won't be needing you anymore."

We all watch. Firmly, he places his foot over the goblet of gold before crushing it into the earth. The queen next comes and stands by the king with the two looking upon one another.

"My queen!"

"My king!"

They kiss and the kingdom again rejoices.

Then all at once, a sudden release of power from the remnants of the goblet causes a strong wind to stir.

There is the sound of a high pitched note getting louder; 'til there is a sort of popping noise. Then faint voices of spirits can be heard whispering upon the wind:

"We're cast out, order everywhere! Let us leave this place of grace, as Christ's honor restores with light and overwhelms."

The Great One then sends a wind, blowing them within a dark cloud of confusion, towards the enemy camp. They feast before the battle while the spiritual spell, from the cup, has travel.

I turn to my father, "Pray with me and anyone else who wants to know our Christ. For His power to love in the midst of every storm truly holds all together in life.

Say with me, 'Jesus I believe in my heart Your Father has raised you, as living seed, alive from dead. You pierced the dark veil, which had held my mind. Be my Great Savior and hold me to grow eternally in Life. I renounce all spirits that abuse outside Your presence of doing right. I surrender myself to the promise of being grafted within Your Vine, which reproduces living fruits by light...'"

I pause and take notice that during prayer there are sounds of hoof beats. This causes me to look upon a man, who was assumed to be working at the stable; he slips away while walking his horse towards the castle gates.

"...Teach me guidance and how to speak according to thy will. Knowing we are just starting to learn that You are goodness itself: Mercy, kindness, gentleness, all in this world are from You Son Of God.

Thank You for Your love that says I'm worth something more than what I've known; as this truth brings peace for me in all."

Prince Liam, raises his hand and continues. "In Your presence, I am brought together by such light shining upon my many scattered pieces. I'm grateful to You for healing me from only living in fragments while not whole. I now trust in Your timing Jesus. Bring change oh Great one, my divine Savior, Amen."

The king, queen, Prince Edward and myself, all come together.

My father, now filled with the joy of Salvation's life, comes to realize his dark deeds against our Lord. He asks us with tears in his eyes to forgive him for all the wrongs he has committed. Then shares: "The price of having a sound mind is everything comes into focus; then it is time to clean house. Believe me when I say that I'm thankful for this grace. I truly have wronged you all, and I am sorry."

There is a pause that turns to silence between him and his subjects. In this new light, I am able to see him in his helplessness, as he bears the fruits of true repentance.

"I forgive you father!"

After our eyes meet, we next meet with most powerful embrace.

"My father, we must talk everyday to make room for our love to grow." Our light of depth from complete reconciliation shines forth to all. The subjects begin to applaud, and seeing the sheer beauty of our countenances, they too become aglow.

My king takes a step back, and looking into my eyes with a fresh fire rekindled. I sense him enter my soul. He then speaks his heart: "I agree! A real family comes together even though each of us has had disagreements. For love allows us patience with each other 'til the truth be known."

"Good, full reality is granted to those who surrender to the living Lord. As The Great One allows for a heritage of enjoyment, which finds a peace that contains love to heal anything greater than our differences."

Edward and my mother join us with tears of joy and forgiveness of their own.

Edward gives me a peculiar look. "You are the deliverer, aren't you?"

"Only by the Great One's grace." I chuckle.

We both have a laugh over the fact that I am the deliverer. It is so good to receive my brother's affections again.

Then, when all quiets down, at once it comes to me. The stable worker, I noticed to slip away, quietly with horse, during my prayer; for all to meet the Great One.

It's remembered that I've seen him in Orth. Why, it was the very one who had invited me to have a meal with Shacha his king. He must be a spy.

Perhaps, the Great One's light now shines so brightly in Calington. The witch is not able to see all. Nevertheless, her purpose will be to work her evil against those positioned in authority over the kingdom.

I will be on my guard, as though she can see, and wait for the Great One's timing. Then His light will direct my path.

It is quickened to me to let the spy give report. For any report he could give would undoubtedly spread fear throughout the enemy camp.

My father reads from a parchment that was just dictated to the scribe. He notices, many from the kingdom have come out thus far. Upon receiving news of what has happened more arrive while he reads...

"With this parchment, which shall be posted my loyal subjects, and I do mean loyal. For I have put you all to the test with my recent behavior.

I wish to clear the air that no dark spirit would cross my heart concerning this kingdom again. The light of the Great One will now reside for all to see in making these amends to you:

I have dishonored my family, dishonored the court, and dishonored this kingdom.

I do not speak lightly on this matter either; for I know I have dishonored my role as an honorable king. My recent unbalance of behavior has brought us into a position of war—and for this I apologize.

The Orthian spy has made his way to the commander and gives report before him. They meet by a break in an old stone dividing wall on a field, not far from Orth. Breathing heavily from his rough ride his words gradually make their way out, "I'd not have believed, unless I had seen it with my own eyes."

King Helca, the impatient commander questions further. "Out with it man!"

"The queen, she walks again, the dead raised! The king restores his honor even now. I tell you, they serve a living God that can never be defeated!"

The commander, King Helca, grasps his chest and suddenly falls over. He is discovered dead upon the ground.

Widespread fear then grips the Orthian's, as panic spreads throughout the other tribes.

Now that their head has fallen, without any leadership to hold them together, falsehood festers, and confusion breaks forth. The magic in the air mixes with the witches' spells for power. Spirits from the golden goblet arrive upon the wind, and their abuse now begins to overwhelm. Suddenly, the tribes begin battling each other.

In a dark cloud, which fogs minds, each tribe becomes their own enemy from fear. Evil judgments of murder and greed, visions gone blind, as to who the real enemy is? Influenced minds, feed from their own strength, during this most destructive battle. Dragon spirits now drive them on.

Meanwhile, back at the castle the king finishes his proclamation:

"...Now due to the Great One, by His righteousness, my honor has been restored. No longer will this kingdom be ruled with clouded judgment, as I have regained my vision of compassion once more.

Love and truth have come together in balance; where humility shall now establish holiness in all.

I've invited Louis and Andre to stay with us to continue to shine forth the Great One's light yet again.

Straight and true thought through and through. For the good of our kingdom; one mind in all. As, with strength known by love sewn together, we will peacefully endure."

Filled with joy the subjects cheer; my mother then goes over and kisses my father before them all.

Slipping away to my room, although I change from the robe of a priest, the Great One still remains noticeably within. Watching from my mirror, I catch Him smiling through my eyes.

Now filled with glee, I pick up my knife and sword out of habit to add to my uniformed attire. There is debate, as to whether I'll really need them anymore, but I decide to take them anyway. Now, in a more relaxed frame of mind, I ponder over my Lord's truth. It rises up, 'til stillness comes, washing over me in love.

Joy then leads me back outside to share Him with the others.

My name is discovered writ in the *Book of Life* I read. 'The LAMB' from the book, has invited me to His supper, which bears witness to the Spirit I've within my soul. It is by this thought of grace that the Great One's accomplishment keeps me in the moment with Him. It is remaining in His doorway that keeps me whole.

Stilled to recognize, the light of His presence, before receiving a most satisfying prayerful sign of sacrifice; peeled back is the foreskin that covered my heart and filling me now with love it is kept pliable.

Upon returning to the courtyard, I hear a commotion and investigate further to see what's going on.

The king's scout has just returned from Orth. He comes running into the court.

"Your majesty! Your majesty!" Reporting to the king he kneels. "You may rise, what is it lad?"

"Your majesty, the enemy troops have warred against themselves; there's not a man left standing. The battle has taken place; it is over before we even had to fight."

Upon hearing the news, everyone cheers, "Hooray! Hooray!"

The subjects, the king and queen, along with my brother and myself, are so overcome with even more incredible joy; we start jumping and begin to dance. Laughing myself so drunk with joy. I become so filled with the Great One's Spirit that I fall down before Him from the gladness thereof.

Yet in the midst of the laughter, I am suddenly made aware that someone isn't laughing. My senses have become heightened; my discernment, grown, tells me restlessness is in the air. A presence of the witch is felt watching from her crystal ball!

Yet, there is so much to be thankful for. What is happening in Calington today will be remembered by generations!

Though a very grievous task I must undertake. Next, a verse from the *Book of Life* comes to me. "God works all things for good for those who love Him."

All of a sudden my eyes meet with Ashley's, the Monsignor's niece. Truth to truth, in a like minded vision, I can tell she sees what I am seeing. "We must face the evil of this world together by the Great One's good," has our thoughts.

As things start quieting down, I stand to my feet and raise my voice. Lifting my hand I motion for peace.

"Thanks be to the Great One for preserving our kingdom this day. I move that this day should be made a holiday."

My father also speaks out, "I second that!"

He then states, "There will be feasting tonight right here at the castle; it shall be open for all to come. So spread the word!"

Ashley has walked over to me and hands me a note. I read it and nod, it is understood that the witch must not be allowed to harm others.

By the leading of the Great One's Spirit her darkness must be challenged. Then Ashley looks over at me and says: "Where two or more are gathered in My Name..." After a pause I finish the verse, "...There Am I in your midst!"

"I'm coming with you."

I see the strength of her faith in her eyes, which meet again with mine. Knowing they bear witness of the Great One's Holiness in character. I tell her, "As He makes all crooked paths straight it is He who will defeat this witch."

Signaling a servant for two horses to be made ready they are brought to the front gate. We next go to the Monsignor who already has heard from the Great One as well. He nods saying, "The brethren will be praying for you both."

When my brother sees us start to leave, he comes over and starts to walk with us.

"Hey where are you two going? Do you want to miss the feast?" Edward, notices our serious countenances.

I turn and address him with a soft spoken voice, "Edward, it would be too dangerous for you to come with us, for you've not yet been immersed in verse from the *Book of Life*."

I pull out my copy of the Book from under my jacket, "Here study this diligently, down to its roots, and while I'm away you shall not be an easy target for evil."

"Where are you going though?"

Ashley, interjects. "Do be patient with us Edward, when it is time for you to know the priests will tell you. Now go; join the others and pray for us."

"I will do as you ask."

Edward and I embrace. He looks sad while walking away, but I know our mission will be for the good of all. Ashley and I then meet the servant who hands us our reins and we start on our way.

XIII

Outside the castle gates before scattered crowds of curious onlookers, we mount our horses on the main road. There are more people making their way to the castle to see what has happened to their king.

We start out slow and pass through subjects who meander out of the way. It is my thought that this is a part of the flow of the Great One's timing.

We're on our way where we'll turn off at Orth not wishing to arouse the suspicions of the witch. Ashley looks at the fields that surround the castle then up to the sky before turning her head back to face me. "Did you know that love is a kingdom where anyone can own land?"

"Your meaning?"

"Seeing the grounds has just caused me to ponder. That's all."

"Have you any more thoughts along this line.

Well, being around the castle brings many to mind. For one, there are so many who battle to store up, yet all the while they miss partaking in the love of the Great One as provider.

In their ideas of gaining ground, time slips by to additional responsibility of caring for more while their affections pass over what has true and lasting value.

As if bewitched–people are trained to only see what they believe they can control."

I then proclaim, "But cannot see that in their thoughts of ownership, all really controls them."

"...While real liberating love is found to be obscure."

"I see your line of reasoning, but the *Book of Life* says that we are to work..."

"But the attitude behind work should not be about the coin or striving for perfection. For we have success by being known by the Great One Himself.

Work should be about spreading joy around from the love of having found our place of service which I believe is of a far greater worth. For perfect love is what causes us to do our best. Casting away any fears of not being found good enough, we are comfortable in the gift of who we are."

"Aren't we to seek God's righteous Kingdom first and all other things will be added while on His path of light, though?"

Ashley then looks over at me. "The fruit of this kind of Spirit is likened unto when you gave your copy of the *Book of Life* to your brother. It is in the lending of a helping hand to meet an immediate need with a pure heart of sacrifice where life becomes enhanced.

These kind gestures of love are the kinds that cause us to bear one another's burdens, and they as encouragements are priceless. Showing the kind of love towards a purpose that Jesus has given us Himself."

The taste of Ashley's words have more than a spark of life to them. They're of that which ignites a fire within my soul. Cherished!

"I must confess, hearing your words are a testimony that our Great One lives. Your uncle has trained you well."

"He is the one who led me to discover the Great One's light."

"Yes, knowing Him has set all in perspective for me as well. He is a genuine person."

"Once I learned how patient he had been with me, I too saw the need to be patient with others.

He taught me about the Great One's love. For in accepting me, even in the midst of my mistakes, more of an understanding of His forgiveness came. Then seated in heavenly place, a place where I was discovered by His peace, I learned to enjoy life with a little more of Him before much. For when one door closes I am grateful that He always opens up another.

The Great One's forgiveness has no limitations for those who call and trust Him to provide."

"I see this too, Ashley, and all else who seek forgiveness must fully be restored, by this grace of opening doors!"

"When I look back on my past even now, I can honestly say that our Christ continues to be gracious with me. For He has caused me to bear witness of Him from being rooted and grounded in His family of love while brought before all.

I've seen His great and gentle touch upon the heart of others too, and by this know *Him* true…

I've even grown to learn of His mercy. Magnified He becomes, learning little of Him over time as verse-by-verse we are brought to His first created root. It is through the way of the *Book of Life* that testifies of the full truth of Him which all must climb while reading each page.

For truth bears witness of itself rather than getting caught upon any single *leaf* that we may comprehend much more than we are able on our own. Over and time again we find ourselves looking into the image of a completed tree as upon God's face.

For line upon line and crafted within His transubstantiate *leafs*, we take Him in. Where *leaf* to *leaf* the heights of heaven are reached unto the ends of the earth, as in fullness of life we come alive from the bloodline of a vine which has the origin of its eternal beginning before time itself began.

A shield to me He has become. For I have received His words of promise which have joined me to His root where the unfolding of full leaves come before His sustaining fruits. This relationship with Him keeps me joined to His vine. A place in His vineyard where I can truly see others, have put forth their trust, as I did mine.

For once our High King's vision had my sight, there was nowhere left to run once renewed. As brought back to drawing from 'The Garden of Eden's Tree living waters came forth from which to drink. I then knew the vine of Life through my Vinedresser's care by love's sacrifice."

"Would you be my *Book of Life?* I mean, just 'til I can get another copy."

"Ha! I'd love to, but remember, in being the deliverer the Great One's Spirit will be directing your path from what you know of Him as well."

Not seeing anyone on the road, we pick up the pace and go into a trot. It is our plan to move at a pace as to not alarm the witch, then ride hard at the turn off to Orth. It is our hope we may come upon her unprepared.

While riding side-by-side, and seeing Ashley's faith, I receive revelation from the Great One. I've been in His service and the scars I have received in the name of love point back to Him as proof. Then I speak a final thought outloud, "Cuts have not entered my heart as He has been my shield. Why, it is He who has preserved peace where the flame of His song has been growing all along!"

"Did you say something?" Ashley inquires of me. "I was just talking about the Great One."

"Oh."

"Oh! Oh! Oh! How sickening. If they keep on talking like this I may cough up one of my demons."

As we suspected, the witch has been watching over us with her crystal ball, but has she suspected that we're coming for her? King Shacha looks on and nods his head agreeing with her distaste for us.

Suddenly, I find my faith falter, "Maybe we should have brought the guard. Or, even troops. Perhaps the brethren." Then I realize with all of these thoughts floating around that we must be nearing an evil dwelling.

I quiet myself from any racing thoughts. Then settling down with a return to being in the moment with the Great One, I slowly start to regain focus.

Looking on ahead, I see the signpost indicate where we are to turn off towards Orth. If I know the Great One, He'll want to reveal how true His love really is before He is through.

"What's this? The signs have been switched!" Ashley looks over at me, "Are you sure?"

"This can only mean that the witch is trying to lure us into a trap!"

"...Or perhaps a desperate move to suggest that there *is* one as to keep us away. Let us pray to see what the Great One has to say that we'll not handle this situation in our own strength. We must continue to be led of His Spirit." Next, while praying I speak as an oracle: "The fruit of the Spirit is of a righteous nature and is to be sown in peace by those who make peace. As this is *love*."

We come to the conclusion that the Great One is sending us as ambassadors to meet the witch to reflect the countenance of His royal worth so she might meet Him and live. This is the Spirit in which we are to advance. Our thoughts now coincide in the agreement of each other's vision. 'Perfect love casts away all fear.'

Concern for the soul of this witch is to take the place of our fear, but doth it really?

A thought next enters my mind, "Is she not as swine who would trample pearls of wisdom!"

Yet when used of the Lord, I am to stay out of His way.

Then I remember that no greater love doth one have than he lay down his life for a friend. *"But isn't this witch our enemy?"*

"What is the thought that has your mind?"

"This witch is to be treated as our friend!"

Ashley and I then come to the same realization of how fair the Great One is and that He is accompanying us to our destination. Our stress next melts away as now we have direction.

The ride towards Orth is slow. It seems the slower we ride, the more we put our faith in the Great One's abilities. Confidence then grows as my focus shifts towards Ashley. I ask further encouragement, "How is it that you have come to know the Great One?"

"Oh, I was very young when He began to touch my heart. For a start, I saw how much joy that He gave to others through my uncle.

Then at around the age of four, I began to search Him out in prayer. I learned to read from the *Book of Life*, as it was formed. 'I met and am still meeting the Great One by its pages, it has been a slow building relationship throughout many years.' I don't know how He doth it, but the more I know about Him through the root of His vine, the more like Him I become."

My eyes become fixed on what gradually comes into focus on the left side of the road. Slowly, we ride onward. Ashley sees the look on my face as if I'd just seen a ghost, then joins me in my horrific vision.

The enemy troops lay dead, a vast sea as far as the eye can see. Both Ashley and I stop due to the shock of what we are taking in. My thoughts then become my speech, "I've not arrived at a place where I'm ready to go into battle against a witch."

"All of life is a battle, Prince Liam. What we are about to face here, the evil that lay ahead, we've grown into position to stand against by grace. For we've been trained inwardly, how to do genuine good outwardly, and our being here will mean a more abundant life for many."

"I cannot imagine our future children growing into a pattern like hers because we've left this stone unturned!"

Ashley, by discernment, then gives me a word of knowledge.

"Only the Great One can bring about change by turning to Him in patient prayer, your majesty. This liar is attacking your mind like the serpent in the *Valley of the Dragon.* She grows stronger as you believe her thoughts which are empty of substance–

Even now, she tries to hollow out your mind with willpower in place of faith so she can possess it. We must keep focus on what is at hand, the witches salvation, or soon after we might lose our way.

Yet redeemed we will be, and unharmed from this battle arisen. For we are to cast our burdens upon the Great One who sustains upon request. He never permits His righteousness to be moved from within us. This is why we *must* continue to trust Him to direct our steps!"

"I see your words have His light and within this sight there is life. I thank you."

"Then come. The time is now. The battle is our Lord's. I entreat that we go forth in His glory. It is the Great One's strength we go with now and not our own."

"Let's ride!" I go into a gallop and soon realize that Ashley is only trotting slowly behind me. Then I recognize that I'm not only racing ahead of her, but of the Lord as well. Peace next returns as I wait upon her, and now with the Great One we trot on ahead entering Orth together.

As we ride up the street, there are but a few people in town. We are met with no resistance and dismount from our horses in front of King Shacha's palace. Facing each other, we immediately join hands and go into prayer. I lead, "Oh Great One, lover of my soul, go before us and prepare the way as we are here in accordance with Your will. Direct our steps for Your good pleasure and keep peace that our needs be met to discern Your wisdom." I then yield to Ashley,

"Lord, as defenseless children we stand before You. Protect us from all harm. Amen."

We look on each other's countenances and behold we are a glow. Then seeing the expression of how we joyously feel in each other's faces, we start for the door. Yet as we are about to enter, Ashley pulls me back and draws my sword, taking me by surprise.

"Watch!"

She sticks the sword in the entrance just inside the doorway and a serpent arrow is cut down striking the blade while it flies. "Wipe it!"

After doing so, I return it to my sheath. We enter to the sound of footsteps running up the stair.

"But, how did..."

"Have faith. I will take you to her."

Ashley takes my hand and starts to lead me up behind the sound of steps we overhear. Then around a corridor that turns twice to where it meets with more stairs, we pass by many doors, but our eyes of faith are upon the Great One's door that lay open. There are no anxious moments from any anticipation that now lay ahead.

While climbing another long flight, suddenly one of the steps sinks down from beneath my footing. All at once the steps fold flat. Ashley grabs my leg screaming as she slides past, but by reflex I manage to thrust my knife forward into a folded step. Thankfully, this stops our slide while holding on. A panel in the wall just below the stair has opened at its base and some whirling grinding spikes have more than our attention.

Ashley is left dangling, holding my leg just above the turning squeaky points of metal death. I feel like I am being pulled apart and know time is quickly running out.

"Save us, oh Great One!"

All at once the squeaky grinder jams and comes to a halt as the stairs return to their original position. I let out no small sigh of relief,"Thank you Jesus!"

Collecting ourselves, we continue on our journey. Nearing the top of the stair, I sheath my knife. With peace restored by the presence of the Great One, it heavily rests upon us.

Our search next takes us into a tower that is sectioned off with a polished stone wall to our left. There is a door to the right and a seemingly new door in front of us.

Ashley points, "The witch lies behind this door." but all I see is the polished wall. So I go for the door to the right.

"No, not that door. It's another trap.

Ashley then places her hand on a shiny stone panel to my left.

I now have a puzzled look upon my face. Noticing my expression, she fills in the blank, "The witch lies behind this stone door."

The wall rotates while pressing a panel. I push it open revealing a dimly lit secret room.

We find what appears to be an innocent old woman sitting in an arm chair with a plain shawl wrapped around her shoulders.

She perks up from an atmosphere of despair upon seeing us. "Oh Ashley, how nice of you to come and visit us again."

King Shacha is discovered seated on the opposite side of the room. He lets out a hearty laugh while taking a sip of wine from a goblet of his own. Ashley goes over in a warm and loving manner to the witch whom I now perceive to be the queen of Orth in place of the vision of the old woman. *"Wait, am I trying to keep consciously aware of the Great One's intent in my own strength?"*

I next hear the Great One's voice speak to my mind, "Be still and watch, then you will observe the spirits give way to My glory."

Suddenly, the witch stands with her hands wrapped around...around...Ashley's neck! It seems odd. Somehow, the way she holds her is illusive to me beyond my senses. It now seems–too powerful for me.

Next, as I take in the horror of Ashley's fate, this illusion becomes broken. For, from her vulnerability, she tries to break the stranglehold of her deadly demise.

Trading herself over to the most powerful of all love, she has offered herself in coming to the aid of the witch. Even while being choked Ashley trusts that she'll be freed as she has honored the truth and been faithful.

"How nice of you to come back and visit an old woman! Eh! Ha, ha, ha!" In the midst of Ashley's plight, my heart is moved from shock to disbelief, and then deep compassion enters in. With a firm voice I speak to this queen whom now I recognize to be the witch, "Come and take me in her place!"

Continuing in her seductive charm, the witch effortlessly releases Ashley who cries out with pain. Straining her voice from the fresh bruise upon her throat, she says, "Don't look upon her, Liam. For beneath her beauty, hollows lay where many spirits live within a dark and empty shell."

"Why doth not the fair child treat her elders with some respect? Have I not just spared your life!"

Ashley crumples into a kneeling position of silent prayer upon the floor, "…Nevertheless, a deal is a deal. My prince, come over here and stand by the window that I may see you better in the moonlight."

"I've given you my life, now come and take it from where I stand. For the time is yours to act."

She pauses as if there might be a present danger. *"I must still be in the Great One's pattern. This is why she waits?"* I continue to stand my ground and maintain focus of mind.

Where joined to the moment of the Great One's countenance, holiness rests inside bringing wondrous truth that fills within. Suddenly, His Spirit floods my soul.

Then plain as day, seeing inside the darkness of the room, I have sight of full and living verse which remains. I am kept alive through living word become flesh, as there are parts I Know of being one with the *Book of Life*.

"Filled I am, having entered the substance of the Great One's blessings.'

My focus shifts, as I'm quickened to realize *'perhaps she waits to trap me by my words and actions? Or is her reality to be captured by my Lord's affirmations towards me which now has me connected to Him?'*

As my eyes find their way into looking right through her darkness, I get the feeling she's not there. I then begin to question this witch, "So, why do you wait?"

"No need to hurry. I've plans for you my sweet prince." Speaking from seductions, her depravity now plainly shows through, and this further darkens the room.

I then offer her a few pearls of wisdom, "I with you nor you with me have sight of direction by the spirits of this world. For when battling one another for control, only an added unforeseen weight becomes our burden. Be mindful, it is through the Spirit of the Great One's Government by establishing love that all weights be lifted. As restrained by love our burdens are carried.

For the deep outweighs your darkness as truth can only open entrance to His kingdom when everything flows to unify. Remember you not, holiness from the stream of purity sets everything to order. Have you not heard of His word becoming flesh and dwelling among us gives direction?"

"I'll not be ruled. It is not my way to follow!"

"Life is not about what makes us feel good within blind sight. For ravenous wolves there be within the darkness of this world. You cannot see them, but they lay waiting to devour. This is why we all need the Great One's protection of salvation light, through resurrected life, as He is the one who keeps back all that hides in the dark until the time be right."

The witch looks over with scheming thoughts in her eyes, "Now let me ask you a question. How do you know the *Book of Life* to be true?"

"The words of truth of the Great One raised my brother from the dead. They are living and contain the full measure of life eternally!"

"What about all those dead bodies, the Orthian warriors out in the field?"

"He could raise them up if it were His desire."

After sizing me up, she says to me harshly, "He murdered them and you know it. So how can He be the giver of life if He has taken life?"

"This is not His doing! Those men made their own choices governed according to the spirit of the pattern they were in. They brought harm upon themselves due to a lack of light found within the structure of their own dark reality of choice which was not of the Lord's. Thus the reality of the *Book of Life*, which you seem to reject, tells me that you're trying to move me from its pattern that there would be a breech in my protection which I now know I have. I am still on the Path of light–Such trickery as to undermine my faith; those who practice these despicable ploys of deceit are liars. Blindly, you would have me led and others to their destruction. So don't try to sway me, for I know God keeps His promises!"

The witch tries to stare me down, roving to and fro with her dragon-like gaze. She seeks a place to devour me, trying to tear into the substance of my being with what I discern to be shallow spirits of my past fears but having had them removed by the Lord; I know they're no longer there.

My eyes remain fixed on the truth of the Great One blazing forth by the fire of His light. It is the depth of Him in Spirit which now speaks through me against her dark countenance...

"Only full reality is able to give off its purest light. For a balanced mind has stability where love and truth are brought together in the search to find eternal life. Direct a clear path they do, as surely as the Great One has risen from the dead proving Himself true!

He is the giver of life, and from this very same pattern, I now fully understand the *Book of life* as Great One Himself.

He is the gate, entering into time. Not only flowing with life, but able to meet each need back from eternity towards us while in its seconds. For we partake of His faith-filled sacrifice, sewing us to Himself by the displacement of each entrance which pierces our dark existence–and even beyond. There is no darkness when there is He Himself as the open door. Only love flows at all times here and waits to embrace by warmth. We too go out to all that agree to come and bring them within the safety of His brilliant grasp, for as light He gives life."

The witch lay waiting in response as my words continue to keep her dark tongue back.

"Standing, He still hangs. Accomplished in moment where all can be joined as all truth bears witness of itself 'together' at the tear within the dark veil of time.

For tasting motion within its choppy waves the bitterness of death no longer breaks us down in unestablished moments. Now all may rejoice in life as

His light between dimensions across the widths of sands bears witness for all to see. For hearts be pricked inside those who are open to growth in deeper understanding of God's humility.

It has been through knowing Him that reality has come. What is done in heaven can be done on earth. His whole flesh and blood life is inside me by the sacrifice of His living word at this moment, and onto the next. He has paid it all! You know of this root of life, don't you?"

Seeing I am not moved really makes her blood boil. In her impatience, the witch pulls a blanket from off her table.

Its elaborate artwork is revealed, stars from the heavens, signs in the earth; that of fire and water with different patterns of spirits upon the wind... And in the center of this illusion of control lay her crystal ball.

With all this bedazzling array of seeming power, the thought next enters, *"Is the pattern that I am truly in agreement with the pattern of deep reality? Love and truth coming together for full balance in life? Or is it?*

Next, the words from the *Book of Life* speak directly through my mind by the inside doorway that comes out through my eyes. The words of my mouth then pierce the dimness of a dark veil in less than a blink. I speak them out, "Hold on to that which is good and what is evil will flee from you. Do not be afraid, humble yourself in the sight of the Lord and His instruction will bear any burden."

In the reflection of speaking them, I watch them shine as all is revealed in the witch's pale light of falsehood.

Darts of light within her now hold her back. For there is no clarity or reasoning within her mind.

The witch vociferously conjures up a spell: "Spirits of the crystal ball, open unto me the *dark realm*. Give me more power. Now!"

A dark haze enters the room, spirits as transparent figures lurk about. "Strengthen me my lovely darkness that we may share in the deliverer's blood and live forever!"

"You can live forever with the Great One now, for this is what He offers," but she doth not hear. For tuned out by self-indulgence from her own arrogance, she's locked herself into the instruction of a deceived mind.

I try once again, "You're in danger! Don't you feel the stress from spirits of power that control you?"

The witch rapidly advances toward me with a dagger suddenly drawn out of a secret draw from her table which lay the crystal ball. Then thoughts from the pattern of the valley of the dragon are suddenly quickened me,

"Stand firm with Me and do not resist her."

She goes to cut my throat and loudly shouts at Ashley as if in control, she is next. Ashley continues to be *still* in silent prayer.

As the witch extends her hand towards me to do me in, I am not intimidated by her spirits. Watching a finger go first, the rest of them follow as they shrivel back. Her hands melt away as the dagger falls to the floor. Her plans of magic have started to come undone.

"Believe thou now in evil more than the many mercies of the Great One. His love can spark a fire where there is no life. Reach for my hand and even now be restored. Come, share in the beauty of the truth of His sacrifice."

"I can't get into your soul. No place to work evil in that which knows pure holiness of grace. For no greater love is there than one lay down their life for a friend!

Echhh, you are filled with the glory of the anointed one."

The witch starts to shake in convulsion, "I should have killed the maid when I had the beautiful chance.

My darkness, I cannot escape the pattern of my lovely darkness. 'If only God hadn't been so harsh!' Woe is me. I am exposed by the Great One's light. Too strong. Arghhh! He burns away my evil from the love He even now gives you!"

The witch begins to shrivel as the shallows of reality for her in time shrinks, 'til swept away.

There appears a number of dark figures that grow larger in the room. These spirits come out from the blackness of her soul leaving her as she turns into a pile of ash upon the floor.

Now I see what was really driving the witch. How sad, these entities will enter the thoughts of yet another soul through a mere matter of a victim's poor choice.

After a pause, I rejoice at my choice to have chosen the Spirit of the Great One–and fully take in what I've just witnessed. A verse then comes to me, "God resists the proud but gives grace to the humble."

I now see, my Lord chose me to approach the witch with balance to restore that which was off-balance. Yet she chose a lie over an existence of life and got caught in her spun web. Where worshiping eternal death outer darkness is entered beyond the abyss. Devoured in place of the gift of truth.

"*Ashley! I then remember Ashley!* I walk across the room and rest my hand upon her shoulder, "Are you okay?"

She nods *yes.* I can tell by the bruise on her neck that it is uncomfortable for her to talk.

"Let's get you home." Ashley raises her hand pointing with her finger to someone or something behind me.

I turn 'round to see King Shacha still sitting in a chair in a shadowy corner.

"You there! King of Orth! What have you to say about this?"

Coming out of his drunken stupor he immediately realizes that not only is the witch not in the room, but notices her lifeless clothes upon the floor.

He then sobers up and collects his thoughts, "You have defeated the witch! Now I am free from her enchantment at last. Praise be to your Great One!"

"You are not only lying to me, King Shacha, but against the pattern of the Spirit of the giver of life. For through your manipulations which contain no love, you capture yourself by the curse of your mouth. Know you not, I've vision to see the trap you're in?

It is by your own words you sever yourself from the Great One even further with spirits dark. I see them to even now pass through you.

You have seen the outcome of what has happened to the witch from her being false. Yet, still you do not turn and ask the Great One for His merciful help!"

King Shacha persists with his story, "We were put under an enchantment! I swear it!"

Ashley silently walks over and hands me a note she had just scribbled out. I look it over, "Yes, this is a wonderful idea. Shacha, king of Orth, show us your innocence by accompanying us at once."

"And what happens if I refuse?"

"Then you will be banished from your kingdom by royal decree. For having lost this war, what fellowship shall the dead have amongst the living?"

King Shacha reluctantly joins me and Ashley as we exit the building together. We walk about five paces before stopping by a cane-shaped pole with a bell. I ring it for announcement of proclamation and the people of Orth gather to see what is going on. Shacha becomes impatient while he waits.

After the Orthians assemble, I address them thus: "Tribesman of Orth, your king states that he has been under the enchantment of a witch from a foreign land.

She has been defeated by The Great One who will defeat any that do not practice truth.

By His grace of truth, His love is here for you to have...and is available for any to experience first hand.

A part of my honor is for me to inform you that evil intent will bring down this or any nation. It flows and smothers all to death, always channeling back upon itself towards certain destruction. Now, "How about you?"

Look at where your tribe stands from under the rule of your king's deceit–children slain in battle. How often do you go hungry while the king dines lavishly each day?

I offer you a better kingdom, one that is governed by truth that there be balance in your lives. As with clear understanding, you will make better choices in what is a *just* light.

All I ask of you is to forgive your king for his dishonoring rule, which even now I put to the test.

'King Shacha, will you yield to the Great One after having conspired against Calington and consider His way by changing your opinion as to being under an enchantment of the witch?'"

"I most certainly will not!"

"Our Great One resists the proud but gives grace to the humble. Now, let your own people be your judge in accordance with what the Great One will reflect upon their hearts. I then announce, 'By a show of hands how many of you forgive your king for continuing on in his deceit?'"

The hands start to raise much to the king's surprise. When all is said and done, all hands are in the air.

King Shacha whom has ruled by fear is now exposed for the liar he is. He next screams about how loyal he's been. How Orth, along with the other surrounding tribes, had been hired to build the castle but were excluded by my grandfather from living in the kingdom due to their differences of custom.

He then begins to scoff at the Great One while jumping up and down. He is insistent that He doth not exist. That his ways are that of the more sensible nature.

Suddenly, a high pitch sound comes traveling upon the wind and rests upon Shacha. Attacked by the spirit from the golden goblet, he finds himself clenching his chest before falling to the ground.

Now, I only do what I know to do best.

"Oh Great One, considering only himself, I know that king Shacha has ruled as tyrant, but even now if thou are willing. I know You will have compassion on whom you will have compassion; please...be willing to spare his life, as I remind You how precious we all are to You."

There is a long pause as we watch King Shacha's lifeless body twitch a few times before turning from blue to a pale white with no movement. It is quickened to me how King Shacha has met his end by his own choice of pattern. An eternally damned life awaits—being seduced by dragons from the dark. Yet, God has turned all around for good that many would be spared.

For although the Great One's hand has always been toward him in love, he has chosen not to receive His affection and meet with salvation. The curse of the blood oath he had purposed against my father has now fallen upon him. I too suspect the same fate will befall upon the others who partook, unless they turn from their evil and repent.

I next realize the eyes of the tribesman of Orth are upon me as sheep without a shepherd. Now moved with compassion by the scars that I sense this evil king has left upon his people, I turn and address them again, "Tribesman of Orth, so there will be no misunderstanding, King Shacha wanted to change our kingdom and not be governed by its existing laws. We respected his choice, as we will yours."

I then draw my sword and steadying it before me after a sudden jerk, I break it in two over my right knee. It falls to the ground before all of Orth as a symbol of peace.

"Do not be afraid. For the Great One's Spirit is of love. Now who would step forward and receive His mercy, that salvation be granted under the name of Jesus, king over the heavens and earth, this and everyday!"

The people of Orth advance to receive His love by faith. I watch as their faces light with joy over and over again, and possessed with the gift of gladness, they rejoice exceedingly. Most assuredly it is next realized that they are no longer under their old king's rule.

After they rejoice, understanding new depths of love, I ring the bell and make proclamation of my own, "As deliverer, I now proclaim every member of Orth to start afresh as new member of Old Orth.

You are all welcome to dwell and rule your province as you see fit as members of the kingdom of Calington.

You too are invited to be in allegiance with my father king Henry, as new citizens in accordance within the boundaries of our laws."

Cheers go up as all realize they've been recognized by a far better kingdom than their old one. A kingdom to match their new identities. Gladly, they choose its properties of peace over war.

I break up their rejoicing with one further announcement, "There is feasting at the castle and you are all invited. For my father has bid that all may come. Now that you are citizens of Calington, you shall be my guests!"

After discovering the kind of prayer that truly joins one to the Great One, all are brought to a changed life. "I will come!" is heard many times over. Then much praise goes forth, offered up in gratitude to the King of all hearts.

XIV

Riding hard, Ashley and I start out for Calington. On our way to bring all the joyous news of what has happened back to the castle, we suddenly come face to face with all the dead bodies from the fallen armies.

The reality over such a loss of life sinks deeply in. Once more I'm compelled to come to a halt.

"I wish to stop here for a moment." Ashley acknowledges and follows my lead. We pause out of respect for those who could now have been my fellow soldiers in arms, even though they died in battle as the enemy...

I am startled as Ashley starts to speak in a loud tone of voice: "The Lord has said unto our deliverer to remind Prince Liam about these dead bodies. Speak to them saying 'Get up you dead bodies, and arise to inherit the Great One's life!'"

A vision comes and I am reminded of what I said to the witch about raising them up. Seeing Ashley's throat healed while she yet prophesies, I am humbled before the Great One to comply.

I pause reflecting over the Great One's abilities then follow His lead.

"It is not by my name oh Great One, but Yours… In the name of Jesus Christ who is set in authority over heaven and earth, I say to get up you dead bodies and arise to inherit His life."

Although I spoke softly like a lamb, my voice thunders like a roaring lion. Both man and beast leap to their feet with the soldiers still holding their weapons of destruction. Horses and pack mule become calm, but the men, realizing what they're about to do with their *arms* within the new change of atmosphere, drop them at once.

All lay down their weapons and rush towards me while acknowledging what has happened. I discover them kneeling beside my horse weeping. They then thank me for bringing them back from their torment, an eternity of living without the Great One's love just beyond embrace.

Ashley and I pray with the men for salvation; at once we are surrounded on all sides by joyous men. All then swear their allegiance to Calington. As I look over, Ashley is the mirror image of myself. We both are weeping for joy with streams of tears rolling down our face as such incredible beauty has just been seen.

It is from the outpouring of God's mercy all weep. Then before we realize what is happening, we become intoxicated with the new wine of gladness from the joyous reality of what has happened.

We're so overcome with fullness of life, we nearly fall from our horses. After such hearty inside laughter is felt by all, I feel it is time to invite them to the feast. I next do just that.

The desire of my heart shifts for the ride home with Ashley sharing my feelings. I announce, "Those who wish to come to the feast can come along."

Those with horses ride with us as others begin to make their way to the castle on foot. I'm at peace now sitting in the saddle, enjoying all that has happened thus far.

All at once it is quickened by the Great One. The meaning of my dream that plagued me at the castle arrives!

I see that if I were purposed to fight or take to flight using my own strength, I would've been struck down.

True purpose has been fulfilled as I have yielded to the Great One's will. He has fought these many dragon battles while I rode upon His Spirit facing winds. At last there is freedom for me as I am resolved to live within the *Book of Life's* boundaries. The eternal kingdom has been found and I've learned that it starts from within.

If I never had my dream three times and been troubled, I would not have been awakened to finding the Great One's way or understand the meaning of my purpose, for knowing the truth within my heart has encouraged me to receive the timing of His pattern of life.

"I thank You, my Great One, for being faithful even when I was faithless."

I pick up the pace, and while riding hard for home, our new allies ride along with us. There is a good feeling of faith in the air now that all is calm. His mercy helps me to realize how blessed we are. The Great One, through the sufficiency of an extended arm, has brought everything together so justly.

At this moment and then on into the next, we are all found prepared riding into what we are to face. His Spirit will not change; I am reassured with our future because of this. For by yielding to His place, delivered from darkness, only clarity exists where continuing to be consistent in His behavior all enjoy Him on common ground.

On the approach to the castle, we slow to a trot. I recognize the warning signals right away. We have been taken for enemy soldiers.

As we stop at the edge of the field before the castle, I turn to the men and tell them what has happened. They in turn understand how three hundred horsemen might pose a threat.

Leaving Ashley who has already started to instruct the men, I notice that they have begun to form a circle around her to listen to the wisdom of her teaching.

With prayers to the Great One on my breath, I approach the drawbridge and am recognized at the gate.

After noticing who I am the guards open unto me. Once inside I see that everyone has fallen silent except for the priests who are praying.

"I thought this is supposed to be a feast. Make ready for the new members of our kingdom, they have all received the Great One after being raised from the dead."

Next, the Monsignor firmly states, "As once were we 'til we met the Great One."

The people turn to the king and someone shouts outloud: "You mean we have to let those Orthians in here!"

My heart sinks at first, but then my father quickly responds by speaking out: "Let it be known that what was just heard has no light or life in it!"

Some of the subjects quietly murmur amongst themselves.

"Father, Orth is no longer a country unto itself, but is now known as *Old Orth*, a province of Calington."

"My son, you will approach me on this matter."

"I go to meet him knowing what is next to happen." Looking unto my father with the utmost respect I hear him voice his opinion: "Have you gone mad? You know how our government works. We've to leave such matters to the proconsuls who are elected by the people. Only after I hear the facts in open debate can I vote my conscience.

If I were to do otherwise, I break faith with the subjects of our kingdom. Take away their voice and it might feed into a spirit that would lead to yet another revolt."

"As the deliverer, this is what the Great One has instructed me to do."

"So it's a divine appointment! This is what you're saying?"

"Is the price of peace more costly than war?"

"Us talking back and forth like this is doing no good, I will call an emergency meeting right now."

"Then I will go back to Old Orth and help them set up a new government to replace their dead king."

"King Shacha is dead! I did not know this!"

"Father, those men out there have been raised from the dead the same as Edward. I have refused your crown, for we serve under a higher one. You know this. Now, for the sake of the conscience of eternal life…

"These people are going to need our assistance!"

"Do you mean that, father?"

"This is a crisis situation that allows us to accept all who pledge their allegiance to Calington, as they have entered through the covering of grace by way of the Great One's banner and are now one with us.

'Oh, the feast!' What will we do for food? Our provisions are low, and with night now upon us there's not time for a hunt. Would it had been the Great One's timing for it all to happen this way?'"

"Our fellowship is the food they need, but so you will know that the Great One will provide even now. Send forth a servant to check our provisions once more."

Edward stands by our mother's side with an understanding that something for the good of the kingdom is about to take place. He has always been good at hearing bits and pieces of conversation, staying well informed for the welfare of our kingdom which has been a source of strength for us all.

I stand rejoicing by my father's side with an anticipation of what I know is about to happen. Upon return of the servant, there is fanfare. My father looks on, "Tell me what you have found."

"Sire, in all of my days I have never seen the store house so full. Why, there's enough food for many armies!"

My father then addresses those at Calington court whose numbers have grown as more subjects have come out.

"It is my proclamation, 'That under the jurisdiction of my son who is a king of a prince and the Great One's deliverer' that we welcome our newly found neighbors who have lost their king and are in crisis do to his untimely yet timely death, I might add.

I now proclaim that we give our assistance to our new province of Old Orth. We're to establish a government that will share in our Great One's banner. For they to now worship in Spirit and in truth."

There is silence and I sense a hardness of heart from the people. For they still remember the Orthian's old ways. So I cry out, "Praise be to the Great One for these new babes in Christ who have come to bring us joy!"

Then all at once, all one hundred and twenty priests, let out hearty shouts of "GLORY! GLORY!" Again and again they cry out 'til the people no longer resist our Lord's sweet Spirit and join with us in chorus.

They are again brought to remembrance of God's complete character taught within His grace. This brings all foul spirits out into the light, removing them from this place.

We continue on 'til shouting as one. The spirits of resentment become lifted and their winds die away to the Great One's calm. Now refreshed, we're reminded of the flame that ignites our hearts. We all go out to meet our new fellow Calington members from Old Orth, with an anticipation that we are in the Great One's timing.

From off in the distance we can see that everyone has dismounted their horses and are sitting in a circle around the Monsignor's niece.

When we arrive, Ashley is so aglow that we can see her face shining in the moonlight. Apparent it is, that those who listen to her are so enthralled that we are not even noticed.

No one dares to interrupt the teachings from the *Book of Life.* Especially, given to new babes in Christ who as little children are becoming in *tune* with their focus of more sight.

We then all realize that this is the best occasion for anyone to be invited. We too know to join in as partakers, yielding ourselves to the Spirit of this most satisfying feast of all.

I watch Ashley as she finishes sharing words of wisdom. It is very apparent that the brilliance of our Lord's fire is upon her: "And finally take in your surroundings–Be sensitive, as knowing when peace is disrupted is crucial.

Keep in fellowship with the Great One's passionate moment of love towards you. The joy of His kingdom will continue to spark life while your hearts grow to comprehend His sacrifice.

This can be compared to having your eyes on the Lord's vineyard. Sweet it is when within the presence of His fence. Yet, should you stray, He even cherishes you beyond its boarders.

Learning will continue inside the experience of each fruit of strength as found within a grateful heart. This is what *protects.*

Identify with what He suffered, and when this becomes your joy, you shall be drawn deeper into restraints by love. It's better than deceptive sin where hollows of unholiness reside.

So keep your eyes beholding him inside His boundary. For holding you in full embrace will cause peace to have your sight. As knowing how He cares for you, when pressures come to squeeze, you'll be kept in perfect rest."

Smiles are upon everyone about her, as by the Spirit she has become a living *Book of !ife.*

"Contentment from within you, as full wineskins, you'll find the Lord provides. He has an abundance of life where you will find a fullness you can never hide.

I say unto you, 'Best be within the safety of His *fence* or the thief will have his way, as he is always on the prowl to steal the gift of life away.'

XV

Aftermath

Lean not on your own understanding and recognize… Balance holds clear minds while only love and truth are evenly entwined. Then with sight you'll see when visions come divine as light be present to guide your steps and keep you towards a life, burning trim within.

In this way, disturbance of restless visitors, unruly be known when present. Ones that try to sneak in by the direction of your gate of peace, they'll be noticed without fear as you'll sense restlessness from bad attitudes of darkness by their pride. Evil is disturbingly in the air as it tries to get inside.

Patience will prevail, though. Always being revealed as in knowing the way to receive a guest at all proper times. In this way your wine of life shall be preserved and never shall run dry.

So remember to abide in the Lord's vineyard. Be not moved from safe relations, and true training will keep you bearing much peaceable fruits. Enjoy them, there is growth in learning to know this meal, as satisfied in all matters of life you'll be. For where your heart is found, there too in lie treasures awaiting."

After Ashley's teaching stops, it is dark. Yet we bear the light of God's love although it is night.

The Great One continues to provide as many from Old Orth arrive over the next few days. They even arrive carrying torches by night. All are received with warm hugs and much affection. Forgiven and loved, even as Christ first loved.

Everyone enters the castle where the priests continue to preach for all those who want to know more of the 'Bread of Life,' while the feast of healing commences.

There has been peace now for the past two years. Sufficient time for reconciliation. Repentance has taken place in the land as all have been powerfully seasoned by grace after hearing about the death of King Shacha. Most of the other kings have invited the Great One into their lives. God becoming head has enlightened minds and making good choices is noted– The rest of the tribes seem to follow this new found joy.

Now that things are moving at a slower pace, there is time for all kinds of relationships to take root. Tribes enter even greater depths of understanding, but there are spirits yet in the air always trying to nest in the minds of the youth. Essential it is that attitudes be watched.

I watch over Old Orth, learning of the intricacies of their government. It develops to elect a mayor who is subject to my father and king.

Calington has blended with all people under the Great One's covering. There has been an added flavor that has allowed us all to find a deeper meaning in our lives.

It took time, but through the conscience of the *Book of Life,* we have learned to plot a course of searching out the Great One in prayer.

As grateful to our Lord more than our own troubles which so easily beset us, hearts are healed. Further, we discover a humility that gathers us to listen around the depth of a holy throne.

Comforting, as He guides upon level ground. His balance is true and no longer do we slide into experiencing unnecessary pains. Friction, on a journey of a free will of servitude, doth not interfere when love is near.

I've discovered growth during healing revelations. He brings us to unity within Himself. As heard, all level off and find peace while climbing His Mountain.

A most valuable lesson has been sighted, too: *"We are not to look upon each other outside of the Great One's light, for His eyes teach us His patient love above all else. This is where I'm found to keep my gratitude alive. I enjoy Him breathing life inside."*

We continue to grow to praise Him in both times of surplus and deficiency, always He is made known within our means. The abundance of His life is found within a firm foundation. There is patience of grace in place of restless strife; I know Him.

I watch Ashley grow mightily. She ministers along with myself and the brethren. Great needs within the land are being met. Many priests, planting seeds, have found their way throughout Old Orth, causing it to thrive.

Other tribes, which see them flourish, now start giving extended invitation. Especially after witnessing our reflection of the Great One's genuinely warm character, all except the Nomads, but I believe within the Great One's timing they too will come around.

Edward and I have grown even closer. We compliment each other under the Great One's leading in so many ways. We share in the patient sufferings of Christ together as seen in the reflection of each other. Yet we continue to encourage.

Our many missionary trips, remind, how patient 'The Great One' has been with us. It is always a delight to be in my brother's presence, there is such wealth between us.

I've also kept my commitment to talk with father every eve whenever at the castle, much work has been accomplished in building our relationship.

My mother is radiant with joy and I rejoice in her happiness. All is in accordance with the picture of completion of the Great One's grace.

Now, so much has been happening here in Calington. I have not recognized the changes within the kingdom of my own heart which the Great One came to establish.

Then it is quickened me, *"I've been giving out too much of myself lately. Though I must be cautious not to close the door upon others by taking up agendas, or I will not be able to receive fellowship to better understand my own personal growth from others.*

Though, when I slow down and remember my bed is still being kept at the monastery, joy fills me to overflowing. Next, reminded of God's peace, which carries me, I observe my desires gradually change to consider the future.

My Great One has so richly blessed me that I'm grateful of His love enough to remain with Him forever."

Now things are happening that seem strange. *"As of late, I've been noticing Ashley in a sort-of-different light. I can tell her anything. Yet, now I suddenly wonder if she is noticing me. I mean, beyond the deliverer and princely priest, doth she notice how close I sense we've been growing together these past few years?"*

I'm reminded in my spirit of His glorious glories and give adoration out to the Great One in song. Praises go up to the heart of my God. Found am I, rising upon sweet melodies of His love all the more. I sing as a bird set free from its cage. Rising higher and higher 'til found upon His intimate stair, which lifts me unto dwelling with Him in safety. Just to understand even more of His grace where I'm left with fuller measures of His eternal embrace.

Learning how The Great One has given me purpose in these changing times, I am found to know His surety.

No longer different roles are there to play. Though, have I truly been shaped to always know mine?

Even within my madness of trying to figure things out at times or taking matters into my own hands, I've prayed to this conclusion where I know all will unfold:

"It is a simpler thing to watch a flower bloom and enter the depths of its beauty by fragrance, for peeling back its petals destroys layers of life. Yet, even within the timing of such a light, there is the deeper root of His sacrifice."

I believe there's a deliverer in every one of us. We've only to let Him awaken. Search 'til all be understood by growing measures of grace within the glory of holiness.

"Gentle is the Spirit of the wind carrying you here this day. Softer still it brings new life to fallen leaves, placing them where they belong and crafting to protect from disrupted lives.

Let your love for the Greater One guide within all until you find His treasure. Then you will know your purpose amongst the mighty winds contained, bringing peace to every storm where dragons be found stilled by light amongst the midst of souls. Some say the Great One still lives. As for me, I smile at the thought of His return."

Other Books available:

- Living Your Life According to Connecting the Dots by Number
- Poem and Scraps for Healing and Growth
- The Playground
- Love Notes for my Butterfly.

Look for Calington Castle II, III, IV & V… And

others on the way.

www.ingramcontent.com/pod-product-compliance
Lightning Source LLC
Chambersburg PA
CBHW020322180726

47991CB00018B/275